Also by Solomon Deep

Elements

He, Felt Scurrility

Oedipussy

SOLOMON DEEP

Perpetual Imagination
Boston • Northampton • New York

881 Main St #10
Fitchburg, MA 01420

info@perpetualimagination.com

FIRST EDITION

Manufactured in The United States of America.

10 9 8 7 6 5 4 3 2 1

ISBN   069260197X
ISBN 13   9780692601976
Library of Congress Control Number: 2015960418

COVER DESIGN BY KEITH ALOYSIOUS SOERTSZ

oedipussy

or
The Last Great Grunge Band of All Time

For

minxy Rotten

With strength and art

Chapter 1

The cracklehum of the Marshall amplifier engaged, and a buzz responded as I shoved the guitar cable into the jack. The other end was snug in my Fender Stratocaster, shiny and polished with layers of wax and buffout that I massaged into the jet black enamel. She was the new, squeaky plasticene right hand of my idolatry.

Jenny watched with a hopeful pride. Steve ate an apple. Kurt sat impatiently, his eyes skeptically darting in his head. They'll see. The only person who was not with us was our drummer John, serving out the rest of his shift at Chucky's Pizza Circus by shoving slices down the gullet of five-year-olds as they worshipped an ironically gyrating fuzzy costume character swinging a useless guitar to canned kids music.

My fingers glided up her strings. A buzzing crunch

cackled as my fingerprint ridges grated the coiled E string. I grabbed my pick off the top of the amp, an orange tortoise shell with a turtle caricature smudged with sweat. It would be worth money someday. I lifted my arm, and the craned necks of my teenage audience extended toward me like baby robins waiting for regurgitated wormmeat. My guitar and sound waves were about to feed their ears in the hushed tableau of this first moment.

I formed a G chord.

My hand descended.

The cacophonous crackle emitting from the Marshall half stack was a stab in the ear. One of my fingers let go of the A and landed on the D, and the life of the moment was flattened as flat as the flattest note as the deflated chord grated our ears. Discord landed on the eyes and faces of my audience, amateur respondents of the mess of sound.

"Wait. Wait," quickly trying to save the moment with a reset. Silence the strings, reposition my fingers, and lift up the pick. Before I could strike, clumsy left hand fingers depressed the wrong frets, and sour notes whispered from the Marshall woofers.

"Wait. Wait," and my audience began peeling from the room, beginning with the skeptic, and then leading down to the only person that wouldn't have minded no matter what I created. Steps up the basement. The room dwindled to my lovely woman.

"Wait, wait-" and the solid door slammed.

It was beautiful as I played it before, but beauty

disintegrated in front of me. It was potential beauty. Jenny looked at me with a smile, and an acceptance of my art, and a moment of clarity and belief that I could do anything.

Fame fantasy feigned the fake future of friends. I wasn't Anthony Kedis. I wasn't Kurt Cobain. I was Todd from Twin Falls. Keep imagining, Todd.

"Show me your song." Patient tenderness dripped from Jenny's words. She was my biggest fan - my only fan. A fool.

"I don't really feel like doing this right now," I responded. The time to make my guitar scream was ten minutes ago without the 'wait, wait,' but rather the wail of a Hendrixian fire-solo.

"Do it for me?" Her eyes communicated the love her patronizing words lacked.

"Maybe later." Can't blame a guy, after all.

I stood and powered down the amplifier, and the electric hiss and warm hum tapered off as the vacuum tubes discharged. The sound it made as it powered down was an auditory representation of the simplicity of the fabric masking over the speakers, and everything else was silence.

I walked Jenny upstairs from the basement and opened the door into the kitchen.

"Where did your friends go, Todd? Did you have a good rock group meeting?" My mother met us in the kitchen, her words and concern waxing ignorance. I imagined her telling me that my mashing of my guitar strings in front of my friends being 'just like Run Miccy D's rap song! You sound like Kurb Kurbain!'

"No, I screwed up. I'm going upstairs with Jenny."

"Oh, I am sure it wasn't so ba-"

"It was," and I turned to walk around the corner. As I walked away, I heard the conversation between mom and Jenny continue without me.

"Well, it is nice to see you, Jenny. It wasn't that bad, was it?"

"No, he didn't really end up playing. They got bored and left. I liked it. He is a really good musician."

"I keep telling him! So much time and money..."

Their voices drifted into nothing as I closed my bedroom door. I could hardly stand their relationship, but it was good for Jenny who didn't have a mother around. She needed time with women other than our teachers.

I walked to the corner of my old 386 computer that I dug out of the garbage somewhere with a matching monochrome monitor. It could only do a few things - it could work as a word processor, a compiler for programming, and run basic command line abandonware. In the world of Windows 3.1, it was from the ruins of Pompeii. I kept it because it was a great way to do some basic writing besides my school work with a small journal file. No distractions of chat rooms, solitaire, or minefinder.

I booted it up, and the command line winked at me repetitively. I typed in 'trivia_challenge.exe,' and a bit-bleep-bleep-boop tune announced the beginning of the game. I toggled the sound once the game started with a quick ctrl-s, and I pressed play on my CD player on the dresser next to the CPU.

The mesmerizing hook to 'Head Like A Hole' began

playing. I stopped the disc and quickly switched it with Pearl Jam's *Ten*, knowing that Jenny would be on her way up once she finished with mom.

This was our relationship.

Our time together after school was routine. We would come home. I would practice guitar while she watched and read. When that got old, we would go to my room as my mom got ready to go to work her night adult education classes at the beauty school.

We would play this stupid black and green trivia game. In between the questions we have seen countless times, we'd talk, listening to music, and groove to the repetitive secondary activity. We were stimulated simply because our life was predictable and safe.

I beat her every time. After each game, we would have a celebratory make out session where I would get to take her shirt off and play with her boobs while we kissed.

"Yay! Trivia!" She entered with enthusiasm and exuberance for the return back to our regular routine. "Oh, I love Pearl Jam... Your mom wanted to know if you needed anything for when she goes to the late supermarket when she gets out of classes."

"No!" I shouted. I didn't mean to yell into Jenny's face, but I was sure mom heard it. Moments later, the slamming front door shook the house.

Jenny beamed. We were alone. She dove to the carpet in front of the computer. Her body smelled fresh, and I watched as she nuzzled herself into the carpet like a pet.

We chose our respective game pieces - two different characters that were different bizarre blotches of boxy greys. Different patterns of boxy grays. Blocky boxes of shades of monotone that represented our digital avatars circa 1988.

"I really thought you were great, Todd," Jenny remarked. Our routine was so predictable that we hardly needed to pay attention as the game started.

"No you didn't, I didn't even do anything."

"No, really. I have seen you play. It's fine - you'll get it."

"Let's just drop it."

The questions came up on the screen and we moved around the board, the virtual dice-rolls and depth of questions managing to favor me. The familiar questions helped my score, exponentially increasing with my tenacious short term memory.

We finished the first game in fifteen minutes. I won.

Jenny pouted, sat up, and crossed her arms. I crawled over her and started to kiss her, taking advantage of my predictable reward for winning and her reward for putting up with her defeat. I opened her flannel button-down shirt. Her breasts were held up by my favorite front clasp bra, bordered by lacy taupe. I never understood how to unclasp the thing, so as I kissed her chest and licked down her neck feeling her breathing increase with intensity, I was also able to drink in the eroticism of her unclasping her own bra and freeing her amazing breasts. I loved watching her do this, offering me her youthful and enthusiastically budding voluptuousness. In these moments I often fantasized that we had moved out from my mother's house already and this was our independent freedom to indulge in our sexuality as often as we wanted.

I sucked, and kissed her mouth, grabbing, and her hands traveled over my back and down to my waistline.

And we slowed. And we began another trivia game. And another. And our afternoon bled into listening to the album in the CD player four times between five or six trivia rounds, shirtless after the first round. And then we napped in my bed.

All I could think about as I lay, staring at the ceiling with Jenny's head on my chest and her nipples digging into my ribs, was how to get the band back together after today's crap performance and blow them away with my music. Sure, we weren't a band yet and they haven't heard any songs, but I wanted to be worthy of them. I wanted them to desire making music with me. Hunger for it. Need it like orgasm. It seemed that I only had one more chance to get everyone together to watch me play before I lost them entirely.

Chapter 2

"Mr. Keefe? My question was about the effectiveness of Bill Clinton's original campaign in the presidential race leading up to his election in the current American climate."

The problem with my plans over the following week was the six teachers I had to see every day that probably disagreed with the way I spent my time. I had one week to improve my playing, practice my songs, and rewrite them so that they were suitable to share with my bandmates... At the same time, I also needed to show Jenny just how passionate I was about her.

I looked up at my history teacher from the lyrics in my little notebook.

"I really don't know."

"Okay, let's just revisit what we were just discussing."

"Saxophone," I responded before he could continue.

"Saxophone?"

"Yes. He plays the saxophone. Rock the vote... all that."

"Engaging young voters?"

"Yeah."

"We weren't really discussing that, but I think you are partially right. Did you have anything to contribute based on what we were just talking about?"

"He was elected because he brought more people out to the polls - the young people were his biggest asset. That's all I have."

"Okay," he paused. Mr. Woods looked to another part of the room. "David, how do you think that the success of the election was circumscribed to Clinton?"

David's head similarly popped up from a different activity. From where I sat it looked like he was eating an apple and looking at a fantasy novel - something he toted around with him everywhere he went. He only payed attention to his classes a fraction of the time.

"How am I supposed to know if the president is circumscribed?"

"Well, he is president, after all, so it worked."

"I am uncircumscribed - my dad apparently fought with my mom about it when I was born, but I don't think the president is. He isn't Jewish."

"I don't think his religion has anything to do with his getting the presidency - there haven't been any Jewish presidents yet. I am asking about how he got the presidency.

How did he become president based on the campaign he ran?"

"Well, I'm sorry Mr. Woods, but I don't really see how if he is circumscribed or not it makes any difference."

"I think you're having trouble with the word -" immediately Mr. Woods paused, and it was clear that he finally recognized where the miscommunication occurred.

My attention returned to my lyric and song idea notebook on my desk in front of me.

I examined my lyrics to the song that I tried to perform for my potential bandmates. I was convinced that it was exactly what I wanted to communicate both lyrically and musically - the phrasing was four-four rock with a standard structure of verse, verse, chorus, verse, chorus, bridge, chorus.

The words stared at me, and I sung them in my head as my fingers formed chords on my blue jeans under my desk. My failure was simple performance anxiety, and if I was at home - the moment I got home - I would practice until I was perfect.

My biggest concern last Saturday was that I had let Jenny down - I practiced and performed in front of her countless times, and yet this one time that I had written a song explicitly for her I managed to mangle the hell out of it. Or not mangle it, rather, just mash my strings against the neck of my delicately treasured guitar to murder something that I thought would bring this band, this idea, into some sort of cohesion among my friends.

Of course this cohesion did not happen. Whatever is the antonym for cohesion - that is what happened.

I resolved to make it perfect by Saturday, and that I

would ask them to come over again, apologize, and make sure everyone stayed. With pizza. If I had pizza, they would be forced to stay. No one would leave with a slice in their mouth. They'd have to stay and listen.

Mr. Woods continued to harass my classmate, and was still working around my classmate's phallic misinterpretation of the word circumscribe. This place was idiotic.

I studied my notebook. In its own section was a buffet of band names, enough for three lifetimes if given the chance. The compilation seemed endless, with annotations and cross-outs through all of the names, and names, and commentary, and commentary, and observations, and observations. I glanced toward the end at some of my more recent additions...

The NonSeattle Band

PisoPeople

Dicks Jerky

Passing Rough

WW I.V.

Ginger Gymnasium

Howl

The CIA Highlighters

The Tubercucolics

Consumption

JFKFC

Spina Bifida

And at the end of the list I added my newest, a combination of my classmate's verbal blunders of the last ten minutes of classroom debate...

President Member

...or did I mean,

All The Presidents Members

...or did I mean,

Uncircumscribed

..or something with a combination of Oedipus and President?

OediPresident.

I turned back to the lyrics and song ideas section. I needed to worry about winning my friends over first. I needed a better presentation; perhaps start the band with a brand. Begin all in. Buy into it, entirely.

As the bell rang, I noticed that the class discussion had switched to a debate about genital mutilation, both male and female, and the impact it has on the victim's life.

"Don't forget your homework, folks..." and Woods trailed off as I walked away, unsure how I could make a connection between how the president gained his seat and the state of his foreskin.

I stood and left.

The hallway was bustling with students and teachers moving with purpose, scrambling through the end of their day. Bodies swarmed around me like a hive, the worker bees wandering about without any purpose that seemed to extend beyond the small walls of this building. The drama kids clumped into their collective, as did the jocks. Their clothing styles and colors bled together, and among the bodies in the school they were like globules of oil merging in a puddle as the water and other colors seeped around them. I was a tiny drop of soap that pushed the oils away as I walked the halls.

Oilbees.

I passed in front of the library, and immediately happened upon John Xiong - my potential drummer who spent our dire Saturday as a stuffed pizza-toting animal during my poor rendition of my foray into pathetic guitar noise. His family was Vietnamese, and he stuck out as awkwardly as the rest of us dorks. The music, though. The music made up for it.

"Listen, Todd, I'm sorry I missed the first band practice," John began, "I had to work and if you had told me ahead of time at all, it would've been a little easier to get off work."

"You can make it up to me this Saturday." My impulsive new deadline was a bit of a gamble, but I just went for it. Now I had no choice but to be ready in five days.

"I already asked for it off. Not on the schedule. No pizza-faced brats for me." It was both a relief and a terrifying revelation. Of course we would be making music on Saturday. My songs needed to be ready. It was time. "I just figured we'd be practicing for this new thing every Saturday, so...

"As long as your mom is home," he continued, wiggling an eyebrow, "I know I'll be there!"

"Really, dude?"

"Always a pleasure - gotta hit the road."

I half-waved as he turned and left.

Many people underestimate the eighties movies that depict the artificial and scripted lives of the American Teenager. There has never been a more accurate depiction of this age. Our lives. Artificial and scripted. Saying a few scant things, waving a goodbye; I was simply planted like a stupid teenage boy doing exactly what he thought he should do - exactly what the characters in the movie, no, what the directors of these repertory movies thought teens should do. The cheesy soundtracks are still unparalleled, and here I was trying to hold a boom box up in the air in everyone's front yard.

It was cliché when it first happened in the movies. High School seemed practically engrained on my mind for my entire life and so damn accurate for what it was really like when I got here. We rebel for the sake of our society, and wear our flannels and give the middle finger to street signs and start rock and roll bands, but in the end we were the same five or ten scared kids in these films. They were damn corny, and at the same time, damn accurate.

Teenage life in America is a tragedy.

School let out. I began my walk home up the small hill, through the field where the football team played, out the massive gates, then up into the cross streets and residential neighborhoods.

During the walk, my mind ran thought through all my options for the band. I revisited my songs, replayed them in my head, my fingers practicing method in the palm of my hand. It was dirty grunge rock. It was everything.

Music seemed to take shape very quickly as my life plan. Not a very good life plan, but a life plan that was built out of the brick and mortar of my imagination. I wasn't even sure how I got to this point. It was hasty. It was irrational. This hasty, irrational, unplanned plan was what I was going to do to get out of Twin Falls.

I would need posters. I would need to get the word out. I would need CDs and a distribution model, or a record deal, or something to get us started. I would need...

I needed to practice.

I entered the house after my musical dream walk through the suburbs of little houses cut from the same die and repeated, and repeated.

I dropped my backpack in the kitchen, and carefully removed my notebook. I walked down the basement stairs, the slumbery must of stale air swirling around me, and walked straight to my guitar.

Hello.

I picked her up, and strummed, and strummed. I made her howl with excitement. I tore through her bones, and slid down her neck, and tickled the bars over the blonde fretboard.

My practice always began as noise. I would play around in key hammering up and down the guitar in order to get a feel and a fashion of where the strings were that day, slithering my callused fingers delicately over the coiled wires. I didn't know what I was doing last weekend, but this weekend had to be different.

I started with my easiest song. It was the first one I had written when I began learning guitar. I picked up standard musical notation from a balding jazz guitarist who studied at Julliard and now taught guitar, correctly, to teenagers for twenty bucks an hour.

My first chords were C, G, E, F, and A. With a successful combination of the above, I danced through what seemed like a thousand songs. It began with nursery rhymes, then simple pieces, and then with my first stomp box it became a metal play-through of Nirvana, Pearl Jam, Soundgarden, Alice in Chains, Screaming Trees, The Pixies, and I learned tamer stuff like REM and The Cranberries just as quickly. It was all a practice in trying to squeeze out as much as I could from the tiniest thimble of elemental chords. I developed with what little I knew, and had everything I needed to become successful in music.

As I practiced, I began to think about getting a job at Kinko's. At Kinko's I could get cheap copies. Free copies! I could change my circumstances to find success on the business end with a simple, mindless job and loose ethics.

So with a flourish, I ran through my songs with skill and determination. I would be ready with a track list on Saturday at the rate of one song a day mastery if I added a new song a day. A new song, play it until I bleed, and then play through the next song. Live a live mix tape. Play.

Notes careened out of my guitar, and the silent strum of the notes with the volume down created a harmonious echo in the distorted light scream of my amplifier.

There was no one home.

I had the opportunity to let my baby call her orgasm in my hands; she could scream through the beams of this suburban home and make it a sexual music box.

I turned the amplifier up, the dial going from 1 to 2. Nothing. It was there, but not enough. 2 to 3. The small incandescent sparkle sound of electricity moved through the magnets and the warmth of the vacuum tube radiated, but a little more. I went directly to 6, and the white noise was finally recognizably bleeding through the air like a knifeslice carrying the waves of nothingness.

This is what the power of potential sounded like.

7.

8.

9.

I stopped there on the amp, and moved my guitar's dial up to 9. It was the Stratocaster's turn to carry the momentum of the moment. Bass, bass, E String, E String, E String, and an F Sharp, and I dove in.

I screamed over the wail of my baby, a bloody compensation of everything that I lived for. The moment was as electric as the aurora borealis, alone with my eyes closed, and I sang.

He.

He walked away with his/

Guitar in his hand/

His Hair Torn Grey/

Sang The Song/

He waited all day/

The Day to Arrive/

The Devil Held On.

His heart was Grey/

Rotten Meat Pomegranate/

Lucky Little Maggot Pie/

Lucky Lucky Maggot Pie/

Kill time/

Knock it off/

This life'll leave you

With a stab wound son/

The Prodigal One

Killing Time / Killing Time

I felt like I stepped outside -one- myself as I sang, and tore through the rudimentary -two- hand signals of my song. It was clean, ripe, and -three- made more sense than anything in the world, -and four-.

A kept man in the shower/

a kept man in the stall/

a kept man knows nothing/

gets nothing at all.

Kill Time/
Knock it off/
This life'll leave you
With a stab wound son/
The Prodigal One
Killing Time/Killing Time

I needed to tear this house down with sound. Tear it down and rebuild the house and the city with my art and my work and my brilliance to keep the strength and the-

Keep me posted/
Knock on wood/
Know the price/
Don't ask if I'm dead.

Kill Time/
Knock It Off/
This life'll leave you
With a stab wound son/
The Prodigal One
Killing Time/Killing Time

-and four, one, two- open your eyes.
I stopped.
Jenny was at the bottom of the basement steps, and my

fingers mashed a crunchy A Sharp and F and wavering G and A. Cacophony.

Jenny stood, her shoulder length amber hair bobbed above her collarbone. Her hands lay over her mouth, her breasts puckered together under her v-neck, her eyes a golden horizon of surprise and awe.

She bounded across the room and directly into me. Her arms encircled my neck, her mouth on mine. We passionately kissed as the muffled sound of the strings of the guitar scruffled over the knit of her shirt. Garbled mash as I peered out of the corner of my eyes, reached for the cable to yank it from the amplifier, and a pop and a buzz as it was freed.

She pulled her shirt over her head, and she knelt before me, tugging at my belt.

I tactfully pulled my guitar over my head, and delicately placed it on the stand as she worked her magic. I was somewhere else entirely in a moment.

Chapter 3

"Well?"

The tippytap of rain falling down the gutter ticked through the walls of the basement. Three young men and a stunning young woman expectantly stared at me on a snoozy, rain-driven Saturday. John was able to gather everyone together and get them over to my house to try again. No work. No excuses.

Jenny wore a tank top, loose sweatshirt, jeans, and thigh high boots. I wanted to send her ankles above her head so I could have a better look at those boots.

John Xiong sat on a milk crate surrounded by his deconstructed drums. Moments earlier we had darted through the rain to transport them into the basement through the bulkhead. He wore a white tee with pegged sleeves and black jeans. He was strikingly masculine, with a quick appearance with close cropped hair and the air of Asian sophistication about him. You could tell who he was long before you learned about his advanced placement calculus courses. He was a focused and driven young man; a bit outside of the definition of anti-establishment, but the kid knew how to play the drums.

Kurt Lobel was on the floor with his legs splayed in front of him, a mop of hair, a flannel, and Chuck Taylor All Stars beneath torn jeans that seemed to unravel off of him. He was a cliché - everything that The Gap considered its targeted customers, even though he didn't seem to notice. His army surplus backpack lay beside him, matching his bored countenance.

Kurt was my lead guitarist. I needed him, and it was difficult to keep our relationship going because of his fickle nature. He needed me, too, but we needed to keep a distance of only professional talk and time together. It was a relationship of interested disinterest, or a cramped awe - worshiping his work, but at the same time pleading a distinct hatred for the crap he asked me to critique. He was a prima donna. He was that girlfriend who asked if she looked fat in something, but you knew that there was no correct answer that wouldn't lead to a fight.

Standing behind all of them was Steve Harvester, funk-bassist extraordinaire. He was thin, and stood as a confident, quiet man. Chinos and a matching straw fedora-type thing over his short-cropped hair, Ray Bans, and grey eyes that were diminished and shrunken by their hefty lenses. He looked cool.

Cool like a bassist. Clean and sharp, he visually vibrated tasty beats.

This was my band that had not been formed yet.

I hadn't a moment to waste.

Amp 9.

Strat 9.

Hum, click, stomp the box, and rock it.

I pulsed through the first song energetically, and a rainbow of hard sound coursed through my arms, to my hands, and massaged through my shiny black appendage, kicking the rock to their faces in waves of pulsating sound sound sound, and grunge, fuzzy grunge.

This was alternative rock, and the tip off of the future self as I rocketed my art into the stratosphere of their minds. Jenny beamed with her fingers in her ears, Steve was focused, John tapped his fingers and feet planning the beat, and Kurt was as stolid as ever as he listened - never anything to indicate any semblance of excitement, joy, sadness, or fear in his face.

The last chord resonated through the speakers in a fuzzy hum.

They stared, waiting for me to say something. I thought, even lacking accompaniment it was perfect this time.

"So, that was the first one..." It was hard to sound confident when the reaction I was looking for was so subjective. They stared. "I have been hitting that for a while now - felt terrible that I really messed it up last time, but this time I nailed it... I have four more. So, I guess the real reason I brought everyone together was this - this is my proposal to you. This sound. I want to start a band with you guys, and I know we can do it."

"We're seniors in high school, man." Kurt stepped on opening the first volley into the conversation. He continued, "What do you expect us to do?"

"I expect you to play guitar with me, Kurt." I responded matter-of-factly and truthfully, "And John, you play the drums, and Steve you play bass."

Moving down the line of friends sitting around, my eyes landed on Jenny. "Jenny, you can't play anything, so..."

"It's ok, I'm just the eye candy."

"Exactly. You're our first album cover."

Furrowed brows surrounded me as I examined everyone in the circle thinking about their membership in this new tribe.

After this moment of inviting them back to watch me play, I realized that I really hadn't spent much time with them at all.

When Kurt first came up to me in the hallway two months earlier it was to talk guitar. He begged me to come play with him at his house. Or, was it listen to him play? A week later in a run-down ranch with cinderblock furniture and a shabby mattress on the floor of his bedroom, he strummed and plucked a little on a Les Paul. We talked about music, our training, and compared our chops when he gave me a go on his beautiful guitar.

I knew John the longest. He worked at the movie theater

at the little strip mall. Our first bonding was joking about the name of the plumbing supply business in town, Twin Screw.

Where did Steve come from, though? I only spent a total of three hours with the guy, one of which he watched me mash my guitar strings. I senselessly illustrated a monstrously insane, ridiculously inane lack of talent.

He came via Kurt.

If there was one thing that stood in the way of our success, it was Kurt's simple, predictable cynicism. It was obvious that we were all about music and our talents, but our relationship didn't extend beyond that. The band was simply the next logical step in the friendship of the four of us. But what I didn't get was, why was Kurt was the first person to speak up?

"Listen, man," I responded to Kurt, "this is what it is all about - this is why we've come together! Why did you drive Steve here? I don't know the guy - and I don't know how you know him. Where does he even go to school?" I turned my gaze to Steve. "Are you even in school, or are you in college or something?"

"I go to Saint Lawrence's - I'm a senior too," Steve replied. He was clearly unsure of the resulting confusion everyone had, and clarified, "home of the Fighting Briquettes."

"The Fighting Briq - never mind." I felt like I needed to sell it more, but not lay it on so thick that I lost sight of the goal. I needed to get everyone together in order to start a band. That goal would be lost on Kurt and his disquieting, muffled emotional clarity. "Listen, I have a whole business plan."

"A business plan?" John asked. "Let's hear it."

"First, we practice once a week - whatever day works for everyone and that we can all get together without there being some sort of exception to the rule. This would be our sacred time. Next, I am going to go get a job at Kinko's so we can get copies and flyers and whatever we want made up. I'll pay for them. Third, we set a goal. In two weeks we will make up a demo with what we've practiced-"

"Two weeks?" Kurt was stunned.

"Two weeks — we're all professionals here, and we can do it in that time if we are focused. Besides, it's a demo. We can screw it up as many times as we want."

"Two weeks..."

"-and I will buy the recorder. Eight tracks, isolated. We can do this."

"...ok?"

"Then, in that time I'll try my best to make some contacts." I started talking very quickly. "I don't know how, but I will. And I will have people at the clubs around here to take our demo tape - all of which I'll pay for - and listen to it, and get us some gigs. Then we'll play."

They looked at me with wide-eyed astonishment and disbelief. The questions swam in their eyes, and their hair-tosses, and the shifting of their Doc Martens.

"So, okay, so let's say we take this on, no biggie, right?" The commas dripped out of Steve's mouth. "The one thing that my folks are killing me about is college. SATs. Getting everything all set. What about that?"

He seemed to be the only dissenter in that category.

"Well, do your college stuff."

"Then what, though?"

"What, what?"

"Okay, so when am I going to do that and all my school work?"

It was clear that I would need to sell the idea to them individually.

"When you normally would. This is one night a week."

"I don't know..."

"Don't know what? No, this won't stand in the way of any of that. Trust me."

"I guess..."

"Why are you here, then?"

"To play music."

"Then, let's play music!"

The logic was almost pristine, colluding with the intense rush of simplicity. Let's. Play. Music.

There were times that I would find myself saying that there was a method to my madness - my irrational impulsive drive to do something huge and stick with it. Up to this point, however, I would create, synthesize, and manufacture without much rhythm or drive.

This time, I wrote a few songs and had them entirely constructed. I just needed a group - a band of brothers that were willing to follow my guidance and leadership into this unknown. We were everything that the future held for us, and it was all in the sound, waves, and a brilliant display of humanity and focus on the jumping-off point of our freedom and adulthood.

"Then," Kurt spoke with an impulsive clarity and promise, "let's stop talking about it. Let's make music."

In a moment Jenny squeaked with delight, unable to hold back her emotion for this moment of enthusiasm and camaraderie.

"Let's meet back here for the first practice in one week. Same time. Let's do it in the afternoon so everyone can work, or whatever with their night." My leadership and diplomacy was staggering, fresh, and outside of my character. This was my dream coming to life. "John, do you want to set up your kit and lay down some beats for this stuff before you go? Get some of it done today?"

"Let's do it."

"You guys can stay if you want – it's up to you."

They stared back at us, but didn't seem to know what their plan was. I called to order the pizza, and we all helped assemble John's drums. We ate. Steve and Kurt stayed to listen to my remaining songs and observe the work we did. They listened, studied, and we moved forward.

John and I worked through all of them, only missing the bass and the solo guitar accompaniment.

This was the beginning of our first practice. Tickled with energy and drive, I focused for our future in these first moments. I was protecting my future with a barricade of sound. So started an invisible wave-barrier of freedom, experience, and a wholesome heartbeat in rock and roll.

Chapter 4

The modem squealed, cracked, rushed, beeped and whooshed. The newer computer our family shared in the living room opened a connection to America Online.

"Welcome... You've got mail!"

A variety of screens came up - email, notifications of the latest news stories, notifications of the comments that had recently been made in my groups, chat rooms with conversations to catch up on, and my friends that were online.

This was now a mess of information that was no longer of any use to me. I was a slave to popular culture for so long. I remember having live discussions online with my friends from all over the country about who was going to win the MTV Music Video Awards as they aired, as if this was any indication of true art in the world. It was as if this approval was exactly what I was looking for - some sort of vindication of my tastes in the scheme of the world and the eyes of some faceless, unnamed "judges." These conversations would go on for ages, as if they mattered. As if any of it mattered.

Perhaps the best of these conversations, the only one of any substance and an approach of a global truth, was the chat we had as Dana Carvey introduced Nirvana a couple of years earlier. I wasn't on AOL yet, connecting to the internet through a dialup relay service, but the theme of the thing still echoed today.

It was splendid. At the podium, with an excitement that seemed as though Carvey couldn't even hold back his fandom (being his own celebrity nonpareil at the time), he announced, "...and now for all your lawn care needs, it's Nirvana!"

The camera cut across the stage as Carvey turned with a swipe of the finger. His smile showed, regardless of who he was, that he was going to jump up and down with excitement the second Cobain hit the first chord. Grohl and Novoselic began to play, and noting that Cobain was playing the wrong song, paused for a moment. Cobain continued, "Rape me...Rape me,-" and cut off just as he finished up and paused on his E flat down-tuned third fret G.

The crowd was ruthlessly excited, and yet something wrong happened in that moment that seemed to carry a tremendous weight in the room, and over the airwaves, and in the history of the universe in music. An electricity never experienced by mankind before and since. The notes started humming through the opening strings of Lithium, and Novoselic saluted an imaginary flag, or was it the producers in the production booth, or was it the fascist pigs that had run this country into the ground over the past fifty years of propaganda over the airwaves?

It was no matter, because this changed everything. We constantly discussed this insane series of events live over the digital interface of the internet years later. Twenty-eight-eight kbps carried a vanguard of digital words into the future, and just as we wrapped up our discussion of this seminal moment in my sixteen-year-old development, so did the walls come crumbling down on taste and the status quo. Novoselic nursed a wound from his bass slamming into his face as Cobain and Grohl deconstructed the world along with the stage in front of millions of people. All of the people.

They did not a shit give.

Neither would we.

I decided to start the online business of the thing. I clicked 'New,' 'Group,'...and the cursor blinked.

I had no idea where I was going with this, especially considering that I had only rudimentary ideas about what the name of the band would be. Five songs, no name, and a little beacon of nothingness rang through to the core of this ill-prepared crew of young musicians. There was nothing but an idea.

The idea needed some bones for the meat.

The bones were the men and the idea of a band. Name.

Name. Come to this consensus by yourself in order to make it happen. What could the name be?

I grabbed my little notebook and scanned the names that I came up with. I really liked the idea of Oedipresident. Or what was the name of that snake symbol in The Neverending Story? Orin? I quickly did some poking around on WebCrawler for the name of the snake eating itself, and came up with Ouroboros.

The page I read had a mesmerizing definition - something constantly recreating itself, seen as a major archetype to the psychologist Carl Jung, and Erich Neumann analyzed the same idea as the "dawn state." What did that mean?

Could I combine Oedipus and the Orin and the Ouroboros? Oediporos. Ouroboedipus. It needed to be distinct, and easy to remember.

Triple O? OOO? Ourobots? Dawn State? Dawn Ego.

The Dawn Ego.

The Dawn Ego and our symbol would be the Ouroboros.

I typed "The Dawn Ego," and "create."

It took only moments to invite the rest of the band from my contact list into the little group, and I found an image of the Ouroboros and played around with it in my Paint program. Upload. Color scheme. After a few clicks, I was all set.

I picked up the phone to dial John. A loud static hush screamed from the earpiece, and the computer spoke to me, "goodbye." I had forgotten to disconnect, and lifting the receiver did it for me. I dialed John's number.

"Hello," John's mother answered warmly.

"Hi, it's Todd. Is John home?"

"Sorry Todd, he's at work right now. I'll tell him you called."

"Thanks." Hanging up, I realized that this was the perfect transition to remind me that I needed to go put in my application at Kinko's.

I printed out a quick copy of my resume on my inkjet printer, and shoved it in a folder. I walked through the house and headed for the garage to get on my bicycle. Swinging through the kitchen, mom stopped me as she was making sandwiches.

"Where are you headed in such a hurry?"

"I'm off to get a job."

"Really?" There was genuine optimism in her voice. "Would you like a sandwich, or a ride at least?"

"I'm just taking my bike, thanks. I'm fine."

She looked at me with a growing half-smile, the jammy knife hovering mid-sentence. "Well, be careful."

And with a nod and a smile, I left.

As I rode my bike toward the Kinkos, I began to fantasize and plan the next two weeks. We would be all set by the time we had rehearsal on Saturday. I imagined us making the eight track recording, track by track, take by take. I imagined our first small show, and arriving with rudimentary recordings and t-shirts with my design on them for a little merch table. It would be okay if there were only a few people there, because we would look like professionals, and we would bring it like there were a thousand.

It would be okay if everything happened slowly and surely. It was all finally falling into place.

I dropped my resume off at the copy store, and shook the hand of the manager before leaving. I got a coke at the pizza joint next door, and I sat and studied my lyrics and songs as dusk approached. I bought a slice, choked it down with the rest of my soda, and huffed back home.

The porch light was on outside the house when I arrived, and the windows were black. The only sound was the klacketty clack of the gear on my bike chi-chickling off the trees, and the houses, and the pavement, and the swift tickle of leaves, leaves, leaves dancing to the feet of the shadow of Jenny under the porchlight.

She was barely holding it together, as I dropped my bike mid-pedal and ran to her. I grabbed her shoulders.

"What happened?"

"Mom. Again."

I opened the door to the house, swift and sure, and walked her up to my bedroom. The house was dark and empty, and she dropped onto my bed in a whimper.

Chapter 5

I returned from the bathroom with a glass of water, and wrapped my arm around Jenny. She had sunk to a depth of sadness and otherworldly terror, and interpreting her mother's manic episodes was always difficult. She leaned her head into me.

"I'm not good enough," she sobbed. There was no easy way through this catatonic state.

"You aren't good enough for what? What happened?"

"You. I'm not good enough for you. Maybe not now, but maybe in the future when we can move into a little house and everything is okay, but right now everything is shit and I don't know what to do. I just want out of here."

"I understand. Tell me what happened."

"Mom called the fire department again."

Jenny's mother had some issues. She had paranoid delusional schizophrenic issues. This story was one of the four main ones that recurred in the poor life of my little lover.

One of the stories was that her mother had a microphone in her ear. She would call the FBI offices in Salt Lake City or the local nine-one-one to tell them that she was on to them. The police would come, and then she would be locked up and evaluated at the hospital. The next story was that there were microphones and cameras in the smoke detectors in the ceiling. Same ending. Sometimes she would think there was drugs and poison in the water, and take the plumbing in the house apart, flooding everything. The final, and most occurring one, was the fire department. She would call, explaining the house was filling with gas, and they would come with an ambulance. She was the only one that needed the ambulance ride to the hospital, suffering through a psychotic episode in the middle of the night in the suburbs of Twin Falls.

"It seems so real to her," Jenny continued, "that there is someone out to get her."

"Is it the medication thing again?"

"Isn't it always?"

The majority of the time it was as simple as her stopping her medication because she felt well enough that she didn't need it anymore. That seemed to be the curse of the disease, silently whispering the possibility that you didn't have it anymore until you take everyone down with you.

Every time this happened, Jenny was heartbroken.

She sniffled, "and everything in my life is so broken all the time - I always wondered what life would've been like to have been normal, and the neighbors not constantly honing in on the drama of mom being taken away in an ambulance - being grateful that they had everything together, and think of the children! The little children next door!"

"You might have thought the same thing as them, if everything was okay."

"You're right."

Silence, and only the sound of her breathing, and she was beautiful even when she was broken. This was never the right time to tell her this - but she was beautiful.

"When I was five or so," the molasses of her voice synced with the dreariness of her demeanor, "my grandmother - mom's mom - was over watching us one time. Cathy was only one, I think. Dad was at work and mom was institutionalized at the hospital again for a couple weeks.

"It's so fucked up, but I was exploring sex a little bit. As a child I think everyone does it, but there is something about the innocence of the age and the impulsiveness of being a child that we see nothing wrong with it. I had this little inflatable dolphin in the back yard - but you know our back yard, it isn't fenced in or anything and - well, I would get on this thing and hump it. It felt good, and no one was there to tell me it was wrong.

"Until we got a visit from Social Services. They started investigating. They asked if I was being abused or something. One of the neighbors had called because they saw me humping my dolphin. From then on, social services was checking on me all the time, and no matter how much I told them that this was all a misunderstanding - well, however I could have said that at five years old - it was almost like with the world, and the neighbors, and the government watching, there really wasn't anything that I could have said."

She paused.

"I don't know why I just thought of that, but... Sometimes I think that mom is so crazy, and sometimes I think there is no wonder she does the things she does.

"I'm so upset. I wish there was something that would change things back to... But then, I don't think they were ever okay."

In times like this I had nothing to tell her. I wanted to tell her I knew what she meant, but I didn't. I wanted to tell her that everything would be ok, but that seemed empty, pointless, and self-serving. What did she want to happen out of all this?

"What can I do for you?" I wanted to do everything.

"Just be here for me, and that will be ok." She put the glass of water on the side table and nuzzled into me. I stared at the ceiling. At this point, I would always counter her experience with a vain fantasy of our future. Some little dream that would make her feel better and that our future together would be normal and simple.

"I can't wait until our band takes off and I can get you out of here. Just us. I'll be successful and making music and changing the world, and the only reason I could even do that is because you're there. You are the strength behind me. Every word, every note, everything for you."

She looked up at me and her eyes brightened. A silvery half-moon of tears hung below her iris, held up by the shelf of her bottom eyelid. She was beautiful, even in this common, weekly destruction of her life.

She crawled over me and pressed me down into the bed. Lifting my shirt up, a tear dripped onto my stomach. She unbuckled my pants, and then led her mouth down, and down, and down, and lifted me up.

She sat up and took everything off, jumping on top of me and kissing me passionately. I rubbed against her, the damp dew of her sticking to my penis as she kissed and caressed and moved. This was the way of things - we would kiss, make out, and get each other off. There was something different about this time, however.

"Is this okay?" She asked the question breathy and sure, and her voice and her kisses were all the persuasion I needed.

"Yes," I whispered.

"...and what about this?" She moved lower onto me, and she barely slipped me into her. We had never done this before, with one another or anyone else.

I was somewhat reluctant to provide an answer. I wasn't sure what the correct response to the situation should be - even though I know what I wanted. I wanted everything with her.

"Yes?" I muttered it, as she sucked on my earlobe. It appeared that this was the next step for us. This was the thing that she needed to help her out of her situation and her mind. This was what the world needed.

She stayed the night, and we snuck out in the morning before mom noticed anything. If mom had seen Jenny in the house, there was no doubt that I could mention the newest grief in her house and mother would tell her she could stay as long as she needed.

The next week at school was a blur - but Jenny and I seemed to pass in the halls with a confidence and electricity and honed-in focus that made completing schoolwork as swift and clean as a razor. Our next step made the various responsibilities in our life happen with a natural swiftness.

I had the interview with the copy shop and nailed it. I handed in a class project on time without even thinking about it. I massaged out my songs on my guitar in the evenings as if I had known them my whole life, transferred down from thousands of years of oral tradition in the punk rock style.

All of these things became awash in my experience, however, as I wondered how I could sincerely look at all of the great teenage life experiences once the aperture has opened? When making a connection like that with another human being I cared so deeply for? Sure, it seemed like such big things were skipped, but in my memory the most beautiful things that have ever happened to me were a result of this new chapter of my life opening. Sex and music, music and sex, a flower not blooming, but punching open with such velocity that the rest of the garden's spring delights were easy to ignore.

It was easy for us to refocus. Our new relationship, our new place on planet earth and in our histories, and we began to spend all of our free time together.

We began a study of most influential everything in all of history. It was as if the stupid trivia game on the stupid computer in the stupid room didn't matter anymore. We went to the public library and borrowed hundreds of albums, devouring everything. The Velvet Underground and Nico, Kraftwerk, David Bowie, Bob Dylan, Joni Mitchell, Brian Eno, Patti Smith, and oh, oh Patti Smith, The Stooges, The Clash, Kate Bush, and oh, oh Kate Bush!, The Ramones, U2, and more, more, more. There were almost too few hours in the day to explore and drink in the kings and queens of modernity.

To explore and drink in each other.

We also listened to the moderns that were in my own collection that deserved revisiting. Massive Attack, The Smiths, Talking Heads, REM, Nirvana - OH, NIRVANA! - and Nine Inch Nails, and we spun and we spun and understood how to become everything we wanted to be because of everything everyone was before us.

Compact Discs spun, and so our dreams of what we were and would become. Rather than making out by the glow of the old computer, we were entranced with the sound and the blur of epiphany, excitement, depression, and sage advice coming from the stereo. We would have highs and lows. Kissing, and the music, and we soared through heaven and the clouds, and then dove back to earth in rousing enthusiasm to feel one another's bodies and the hum of music, and the scent of skin, and the sensation of every little nerve ending on my lip trailing across it. We would embrace each other, kiss, cry, simmer, and stew as the waves entered the room and surrounded this period of we.

Eventually, the Kinko's call came. My employment as a tentative and dedicated employee of Kinko's began in a week, and I would arrive with chinos, get a blue Oxford shirt, and learn how to make copies.

Easy.

So Saturday finally came around again, and the momentum Jenny and I created with our informal study of the past fifty years of music all came to a head.

In the basement. Saturday. Four men and their biggest fan. It was everything.

John and I began practice on guitar and drums with what we knew. We ran through the five songs that I presented to them a week earlier. The songs sizzled. John performed modifications that he added to his drums, and I presented my pedalwork that I hadn't added until this first run-through. We screamed the songs, and going through them twice we gave Steve and Kurt a solid concept of what the base skeleton sounded like.

Steve came in on bass. We began with "Killing Time," and ran through it a few times as he gained some footing on some preliminary decisions. The lick he was playing with was tasty and dynamic - a safe bet, but not overpowering.

Then, we asked Kurt to add his solos. It was as if he had been strategizing his moment all week. The scream of his guitar broke through everything we had been doing so far, fuzzing up and out of the depths of his being. The sound became an appendage that made itself known to the existence of all of us, an immediate and clear laser shining through the purple cloud of song. It was solid. We all felt the light and the cloud and the song in our teeth.

It was completely new and beautiful.

We ran through it one more time.

"What do you think?" Jenny got up and left up the stairs - presumably for the break to get a drink.

"That was...That was new. It was fresh," John's drumsticks were crossed on his lap as he delivered his critique. "Everything came together, like... Unreal."

"Kurt?"

"We rode that," he said, nodding. "It was nice. I think we have something."

"Yeah." Steve nodded as well, his eyes squinting with introspective delight.

Kurt uncharacteristically chimed in again, "that shit is like sex, man."

There it was. The approval of the men who would be the backbone of this outfit. We were making something happen, and the thing we were making happen was a simple and strategic team art project that would bring us fame, fortune, and no concern for making anything happen but our own successes in future endeavors. We were everything in this moment. The future expanded in front of us, perpetually cascading exponentially forward. This was all we had hoped for.

"What do we call ourselves?" Kurt asked.

"I made us a group online," I saw John nodding, so it was clear he had already found his way to the online group. "I did this whole research thing, and found some incredible images and information about starting anew, and origins, and... Anyway, the thing that struck me was the image of the Ouroboros. It is that snake that's eating its own tail. The thing has to do with the cyclical nature of life, and rebirth, and how we all are part of this immortal cycle. Some psychologists talk about it being part of the awakening self. I threw all that together to make something simple, though, since I figured no one will probably say Ouroboros correctly.

"We are 'The Dawn Ego.' Simple. Straight. It can be interpreted in many unique and thoughtful ways, and we can still use the Ouroboros as our symbol - the logo could be a circle and would perfectly fit on your bass drum."

Everyone nodded, and communicated their love for the idea. John didn't entirely enjoy the idea of defacing his drum head, but beside that it was a brilliant and clear admission that my army had joined me for the battle for our fates and survival. This was the future of our society, and my men were rallying behind me for the victory over what our otherwise poor futures may have held.

This was it.

Chapter 6

And so the journey of four men and the beautiful maiden began with a simple song. Every Saturday, they explored the musical world of their creation as a vanguard of sound.

I found myself working at the copy store three nights a week. I found myself sleeping with Jenny as many nights as I could get away with it - mother didn't say anything about the situation and rarely saw me off in the morning. I was on autopilot in school, completing work and handing it in as if it was an afterthought - but it was educationally sufficient.

I found everything was perfect and applicable and swimming-smooth. I was floating. I was soaring.

The first week I bought an eight track recorder and a stack of cassettes. I recorded the guitar track with my metronome, and the rest would be easily filled in and mixed down on Saturday during the following practice.

"Do you want me to get my camera and take your picture together at rehearsal tomorrow?" Jenny asked me on my bed as we listened to Pearl Jam's *Ten* for the thousandth time. It was already the end of the week, and we had spent all week sleeping, waking, school, work, sleeping, waking, school, recording, and over and over, through and through to now.

"Really?"

"Yeah, I took that photography course. I have a camera and everything. I can use the darkroom at school."

"I didn't even think of that. Of course we'll need a picture!"

"...And I'll be the one to give it to you. Can I take your picture now? I have my camera in my bag."

She took out her big, boxy camera with the lens levelled at me like a gun.

"Just do your thing."

She started snapping, mostly me in profile looking at my notebook and working. The light in the room was dim, and the music continued while I scribbled my ideas. The intimacy of the moment was awkward, and I felt an embarrassing sense of vanity being so central to her attention.

She stood up and took me out of my room, down the stairs, and down the hallway. I put on my Carhartt jacket. We went outside.

The rows of houses in the neighborhood seemed depleted after the winter, and the air was still crisp in that manner that one couldn't truly be sure that the spring had arrived. I tried to make clouds in the air with my breath, even though I knew it was too warm. Or was it? I kept checking, shuffling my arms in my sleeves, shifting my hands in my pockets.

Jenny stood far away, fiddling with knobs, the film advance reel, and the lens as she snapped picture after picture.

I wanted this to be perfect, but didn't know what to do or how to stand. I acted like me, without much direction or care to act like anything.

"Let's go in – I'm freezing." Jenny walked toward the house ahead of me, cradling her instrument.

"Want me to make you a snack?"

"Yes! A snack and TV before we go back to our art!"

We travelled straight to the kitchen. I got the sticky white bread, the butter, and the Martian-yellow square cheese for making grilled cheese sandwiches.

"I don't want to bring it up, but how's your mother?" I never wanted to press it, but at the same time there was a certain desire to show that I cared and wanted to be that thing in her life that was a possible respite, or even a lockbox for her emotional outpourings. I was the thing she needed most; just to be there.

"Still in the hospital." She stood with her hands behind her on the counter, looking at her feet. The camera was strapped around her neck, and the strap cradled her breasts as if to present them. Why was it in the most human times that the most animalistic passions arose?

I dropped the first sandwich onto the pan, sizzling lightly and filling the room with the aroma of cheap butter and flour. There's something about the comfort of a crap grilled cheese sandwich that makes it the culinary nonpareil regardless of the ingredients. It was almost perfect because of the crap ingredients.

"I didn't want to tell you, but," she continued as I flipped the sandwich, bringing the golden crisp toast to the top to sear the opposite side, "dad was talking about separating from her and moving or something... He seems to be getting pretty sick of having to... deal... with mom."

I couldn't bear to bring my eyes up from my task. This was both an enormous revelation and an uncertainty that came with the lack of factual information in what she was saying. Her mom was still in the hospital. Her dad was frustrated.

It was going to be ok, Todd.

A char scent sent my pan hand scrambling for the plate to unload the sandwich. It spun and tottered on the small plate, and Jenny put a hand out to steady it.

"Sorry," I responded, feeling helpless. I put the plate down, buttered some more bread, and she continued.

"It's not a real thing, but... I just thought I would tell you about it for when it comes up again." I dropped the bread and cheese into the pan. Sizzle. "It probably won't."

"You'll be coming with me and the band on tour and seeing the world, though, so we are all set," I replied. I wanted to save her.

"You're right! But what about college? What about what's next for us. I don't even have a plan, but I know I have to have one. I applied to State, and the community college, and I did my SATs, and I have everything all lined up... but for nothing."

"Me too," flip the sandwich, "but you don't think that this is an option?"

She looked at me, and smiled, and shook her head back and forth as her hair danced around her face. She communicated so much in that one simple gesture. She was saying, 'you're crazy, but I love you so much' and 'you are a dreamer, but I love you so much,' and 'this is insane, but it just might work, and I love you so much.'

It also seemed like she was saying, 'you'll be playing music in your mom's basement for the rest of your life, and I really like playing around now, but this can't go on. I will find someone else and it will be glorious because even though I went to college I can pop out a few kids and live off of his salary and it will be a life of routine and repetition and it will all be wonderful. We will die and be buried next to one another on a green grassy knoll, and every year our grandchildren will plant blossoming geraniums and yawning lilies over our respective rotting corpses. We will be laying in the earth, facing the stars, only we won't know it because our hearts stopped beating decades earlier and the maggots had eaten our eyeballs out.'

"I love you, you know." There was sincerity in her voice, as well as the weight of all my imagined words in her face.

"I love you, too."

We walked into the living room with our sandwiches, and turned on the television. We landed on MTV. A song was playing, but the feed was immediately cut, and the spaceman appeared in a slate I had never seen before. Then, it cut to the spinning typewriter ball, then the N-E-W-S stamping on the screen.

Kurt Loder came on and began talking quickly.

"Hi, I'm Kurt Loder with an MTV News Special Report.

"The body of Nirvana leader Kurt Cobain was found in a house in Seattle this morning, dead of an apparently self-inflicted shotgun blast to the head. Police found..."

Our intimate moment turned stifling and claustrophobic. The words coming out of his mouth became a jumble of nothing, cotton balls speeding by with details and figures as our beloved figurehead was...what was the word he used? Dead?

I froze, connecting only with a supposed reality that played out in front of me; an alternate reality where the work of fate and a terrible series of events hung over us, and the weight of the moment, oh, the weight.

The special report cut out, and it was back to the music video. How? How could this happen? The regular feed? Music videos? What in the world was going on? Stay tuned for more, he might have said? A two hour special he might have said?

Our sandwiches remained hovering in the air, a bite taken out of them, and our arms were hovering crane-appendages.

We didn't move for hours. He was gone.

Chapter 7

The next day began with absolute drive and lack of sympathy. We seized every second, we started recording the rest of the tracks. This Saturday was entirely the point of the entirety of everything. We weren't sure when we would be called home, and we lived as if our final moments weren't wasted laying down tracks for our demo tape. Five songs. Electric resonance cemented our voices and sound to tape, forever.

John came early and jumped on the drum tracks. We did it over and over again until he replaced the metronome with an almost perfect time ragged beat. If he was too perfect it didn't sound right, and there was an art to good percussion.

The rest of the band arrived and unapologetically burned through our set as if it was already second nature. We attacked, and attacked, and drove, and recorded, and pushed through to the other side.

When everyone began to mention that they had to leave, I improvised a quick review of our work. I hooked the eight track to my guitar amplifier with an adapter, and we listened.

It was creative, pure, and amazing, and we listened with closed eyes as if this version of the truth was the absolute truth. There was something scratchy and magnetic about the recording - very garagey - the sound added to the definitive grunge elements of it appearing as though there wasn't even effort or time put into the work itself. We recorded it in my basement, after all, and the materials we had at our disposal were a few hundred dollars in equipment and some great music. That was all we needed.

I scanned their faces, a satiated glow radiating as my ears drank the music and my eyes bobbed from face to face. The music was a stone dropped in a glassy lake. Ripples of enjoyment echoed through us, and we knew it would resonate on.

"So what's next?" Steve approached the project as a passenger on this train. We didn't mind. He was a great bassist.

"Jenny takes our picture before you go. She develops them, I make a press pack, and we start finding gigs."

"Do we have enough stuff?" Kurt, the practical.

"Does it matter if we start small?"

Their heads all bobbed in agreement.

We went outside, and Jenny snapped pictures as we posed and moved around in the back yard and the street. The whole thing took another ten minutes, and the guys were able to pack up and leave very quickly. They left one by one, but John continued to drag.

"What are you doing today?" I asked.

"Nothing, just hanging around."

"Let's do something - help me put together the press kits. We can design some stuff and head over to the Kinkos and print everything out - get everything ready to go."

"Cool with me!"

We headed up to my bedroom and started dubbing on my tape deck. I showed him how to do it - the tape deck had a double speed feature, so the twenty-three minute tape took only about twelve minutes each tape.

"So, did you see the news?" I asked. I flipped through some old encyclopedias.

"News?"

"Cobain."

"No."

I tried to remain calm. Perspective was everything in a situation such as this. But was it possible that the drummer for my band was completely out of touch with the business we were in? Were we opening a new church, and one of our priests wasn't aware of our worshipped deity?

Why weren't people crying in the streets? We should be laying down palm fronds as the casket of the once and future king of rock was brought through the streets and worshipped! Or visited in the capitol, lying in state for the masses to pass under a perpetually burning American flag! Something!

"He killed himself - apparently earlier this week -some electrician found his body yesterday. I don't know what to do." I made a motion making a gun out of my fingers and holding it to my chin. I whispered 'pow.' I have no idea why I did it.

"Was he a relative of yours?"

"No, it's just, the thing of it. He was king."

John nodded, seeming to undermine the seriousness of the information I was giving him. I was surprised - some cultural black hole existed behind his eyes.

"Could you trace around this?" I handed him a paper sleeve for a tape case, and he drew his pencil around it on a piece of copier paper, and included lines for the fold marks.

I found an illustration of the Ouroboros and cut it out of one of the encyclopedias we never used. It was the perfect size for our application on the front of the tape. I found some other illustrations: a twisty dragon and Saint George that matched the diameter of the Ouroboros. The head didn't match, but we found two images that we cut up like a Terry Gilliam Monty Python animation - and it even ended up matching my original idea of the 'President's Member' in a way... With a little paste and attention with a hobby knife, we had an image of a dragon Richard Nixon eating a snake Ronald Reagan eating a dragon Richard Nixon and on and on forever. John illustrated some designs around it, and we cut out letters from some old magazines to make up the track names and titles. We called it "The Dawn Ego, OedEPus Demo" with a play on the initials for 'Extended Play' albums.

We switched gears and moved to the computer to type up some copy for the press kit.

"What do you think this stuff normally says? What do we include?"

"No idea."

As the leader, I thought it was my responsibility to take executive action, making my thinking out loud seem a lot more like a solid plan than it really was.

"Here is what I think - one double sided paper with biographies and a little bit of information about the band. We can print a bunch of stickers out and these tape covers at the Kinko's, and then send that along with the tapes. Tape, stickers, one pager, -oh! and a photo once Jenny has that buttoned up. When did she say that would be?"

John nodded. "She was going to do it Monday at school, right?"

"Yes - awesome. I can bring these around as soon as Monday afternoon!"

The computer booted up and I entered 'wperfect.exe' to get into the word processor. As the cursor blinked, we looked at each other and it was apparent we were lost.

We had to lie. We lied our asses off to make it sound like we had much more control and an idea about who we were than even we knew. We typed a fabrication and a fantasy. We knew what we were doing, at least it seemed like we did.

Introducing

The Dawn Ego

The newest grunge band out of the up and coming scene of the original rockers in Twin Falls, Idaho *[really?]*, the origins of grunge are unmistakable in the sound of this brash and driven group of young men who have been recording before grunge was even a thought - as early as 1988 with their first single to hit the college radio circuit *[since we were 13?]*. Playing small venues, their high energy show seems like they are going to lose it at any moment *[where small venues equaled basement, and lose control equaled the fact that we had no idea what we were doing]*.

The band is currently looking toward new markets *[any markets]* to bring their energetic and wholly original grunge sound *[not really]* to any new audience across the nation, and would like to perform at your venue at no cost *[or to just get any gig anywhere]*.

Simply listen to their demo EP and decide for yourself. There is no doubt, however, that this in-demand group will be booked for years to come in only a few short weeks *[define booked?]*.

The Dawn Ego is...

Todd Keefe - Rhythm Guitar and Songwriter

Native to the Twin Falls Grunge scene *[the founder of the Twin Falls grunge scene? What grunge scene? This grunge scene!]*, Keefe founded The Dawn Ego after his other projects The President's Member and JFKFC made huge gains around the United States *[too many president-related images? Maybe it is a theme in my work]* opening in major tour venues in all major cities *[white lie]*. This marks his first foray as leading man, exploring his own themes in his work and leading a team for the first time.

Kurt Lobel - Lead Guitar

Kurt joins The Dawn Ego after playing guitar for a major touring pop act. His creative control over the featured elements of all of the Dawn Ego's songs brings out haunting and expressive melody of the modern grunge movement. He studied with *[can we just make up names, here, assuming the reader will think they are real people?]* Bryan Cosgrove, Butundi Oblundi, and Carmen Santiago *[too much?]* to build his global and intelligent stylings. Official selection of Fender Guitars *[his selection of his Fender Guitar when he bought it is somewhat official to him]*.

Steve Harvester - Bass Guitar

Steve is the newest addition to the band, coming from a classical training in Jazz bass *[whatever that means]* to join the rhythm section that hums below the striking driving sound of the band as a backbone that *[mention some famous people!]* is heavily influenced by Jack Bruce and Les Claypool.

John Xiong - Percussion

"Wait, stop. I want to change my name."

"Why?"

"It's too... Vietnamese."

"It's cool."

"Eh."

"What if we change it to X?"

"Like, Johnny X!"

It was decided.

"What do we type?"

"Just make some stuff up like you have been. I like this."

Johnny X - Percussion

Johnny X comes from a long line of professionally trained percussionists who studied with Avedis *['But I didn't.' 'White lie, we just don't have to say which Avedis!']* and came up with his original hammer-style *['what?' 'I don't know - don't worry about it, sounds more official.']* that remains a striking contrast to many bass performers of the common era.

To book The Dawn Ego for the concert your customers will never forget, leave a message for Carly at...

"That's your mom?"

"I know, I'll just tell her I put our number on there and I'll be the one to call them back."

"Oh."

We wrapped up copying eight tapes and printed out the letter with the dot-matrix printer in my bedroom slamming ink digits into the paper. There was something grungy in itself that we were using a barely antiquated printer - so I kept the guiding hole edges on the paper to see if we could use it on the press kit. I tossed the tapes, the copy for the band, some sharpies, the encyclopedia and cut-up magazines, the tape cover, and everything else into a box.

"To Kinkos?" I asked.

"To Kinkos!"

When we got to the store, we cut and pasted, copied and zoomed and disintegrated our artwork, and print onto glossy cardstock. We stuck, folded, taped, and assembled. We used the design of the tape cover to make a letterhead, stickers, and decals for the tapes. When we finished, we had enough to make up eight press kits, minus the photo of the band. With my employee discount (both of the official variety and the variety of the one that my blue-oxford-shirted friend behind the counter added by accidentally leaving a few of the copies off of the order and returning a wink), it only came to eight dollars.

If I used the color copier to make the band photos rather than having Jenny make photographic prints, we were going to get our name out to eight venues for less than two bucks each. Perfect.

We walked next door to the pizza shop and ordered slices and root beers, and we talked strategy as we ate.

"What's next," I began, "is that we just need to line up some dates that make sense, and work together to keep us driving forward. We start with some small venues, and then maybe try to add a song a week or something, and then practice all of the earlier ones. We might even be able to book, what, a show a week?

"Do you think that one rehearsal and one show a week is too much for everyone?"

"Reasonable to me - I don't know about the other guys. I mean, we all have a job. We'll just have to see."

"True..." Between the Nirvana thing, and the fact that I only knew this young man as a result of some bizarre acquaintancehood, I figured it was time to find out who this guy was.

"Who are you?" I asked.

"Who am I?"

"Yeah, I mean, I know little. I know you're nice, you can beat a drum, your family is Vietnamese, and a few other things... But I want to know who you are and what you want to do."

"I am just a guy, I don't know."

"What do you like?"

"Music. Probably going to go to school for biology after I get out of here, though. I applied to some tech schools that I have a pretty good chance of getting into because of my SAT scores. I don't really know, though. I'm still trying to figure things out." He looked at the ceiling. "I have four younger sisters and a brother who is older than me. Big family. I don't know."

"Do you really not know who Kurt Cobain is?"

"Are you kidding? I don't follow the news or anything. People worship him and stuff, so I don't know. I don't. I make my own music."

I appreciated his frank, virginal self-assessment.

We left the pizzeria and headed home. As we waited at a red light, John hit my arm.

"Hey - look."

He pointed to The Caffeine Machine, a dark corner coffee shop. It was mainly ignored by our peers. The dark walnut and gothic interior was a stark contrast to the bright yellow photocopy in the window that anyone could read from the street. It read, "live music wanted."

"Whoa!" I immediately cut the wheel and turned onto the street next to the corner restaurant, the wheels slightly giving way to squeak over the pavement. We parked on the street a half a block up and collected our first press kit from the back seat. We got out of the car, and walked toward the cafe.

The front of the building was a curved sculpture of brushed steel with waves of curled, papery sheaves and spiky pen-like appendages shooting into the sky. Steel cups and smoky swirls emanated from them in a postmodern gothic and industrial work of art that surrounded the tinted windows. In the dusk, the darkness invited us with radiating warmth.

As we walked in, the interior was earthen wood. I smelled incense and coffee, a creamy green pleasantness that surprisingly complimented the atmosphere. Gene Loves Jezebel was playing on the cafe's sound system on the border of too loud, but we were the only customers in the room. Darkness crept through the city.

A thin man in his mid-forties in a t-shirt, jeans, and an apron leaned on the counter. He was reading a magazine that he put aside as we approached.

"How can I help you gentlemen?"

"We saw your sign," I said, indicating the sign in the window. I put my hand out for a handshake, "I'm Todd, this is Johnny X, and we're members of The Dawn Ego. We are interested in finding some new places to play. What kind of bands do you have?"

"We haven't had any. That sign has been up for a month or so. I want to get more people in in the evenings, and would love any band to come play to make this more of a community space."

"Nothing yet?"

"Nope."

"Here's our kit." I handed him the letter, tape, and some stickers. He put the stickers in front of the register, perused the letter and bio, and turned the tape over in his hand.

"I'm Paul." He held his hand out. "How about Friday?"

"-yes," I blurted.

John had turned to me and was about to begin a discussion, but I was ready. I knew we were ready, and I knew that this was our shot at something. I could have sounded a bit less desperate but it would be easy to call everyone in, or even last until Friday without a rehearsal.

We had no stage identity, and no brand without the artwork on the letter and the tape. We were essentially nothing but the songs - but perhaps jumping into it this way was the most drastic, damaging, brazen, and striking way to hit the scene. If we sucked at the coffee shop, so what?

This wasn't the big league... This was the beginning.

"Excellent. It's last minute, I know, but maybe I could have you in again in a week. Maybe I could have you in every Friday, or we will skip one after we see how it goes... I am not sure how it will look, but you are first, so you are first. I can give you free coffee as payment for the night.

"The only thing I ask is that you promote yourselves - but this looks like you have PR down pretty well. Make it happen. Promote, promote, promote, and I will give you the space and make the coffee in exchange for allowing me to run my shop. I will even sell your tapes, whatever you want. I can keep inventory, and give you your money at the end of the night."

We nodded.

"Great. I'll see you Friday night - how does seven sound?

You can come load in any time after five."

We nodded, again.

"See you then." He held out a menu, likely printed by Kinkos. "My number is on here if you guys have any problems or need anything."

We thanked Paul and walked into the evening, the music dumbing down behind the plate glass. The streetlights and headlights danced over the brilliantly polished artwork of steel, and the store was a golden, shimmering dais. This was where it would all start. It was our kismet machine. Fate breathed into us.

"I can't believe it - this is insane," John said. I couldn't tell if he was upset, or surprised, or as excited as I was.

"What do you mean?"

"We haven't been going at this much more than, what, a week? Two?"

"I think that's how these things work."

"He didn't even listen to the tape!"

"I know. I have a feeling it will all be ok."

"I do too," John said. We got into the car.

"Tomorrow we get the other guys on board. I'll go back to Kinkos and make more posters. I have work tomorrow night, anyway. Then, we go crazy and get all of our friends to show up at the show - our friends, our moms, our cousins, everyone - and we get this guy to sell a lot of coffee to them. Then, we'll have one solid place we can count on."

I turned the car back into traffic. We waited at the light

parallel to the coffee shop.

"Do you think we're ready?" I asked.

As a leader I know I wasn't supposed to show doubt, fear, or to waver in any way. In art there is never a right answer; there is always room for improvement. It's better to fear perfection than to assume it.

John was confident and sure of his response when he said, "I do."

The night was crisp and frigid.

Kurt Cobain was dead.

We were alive.

We only had so much time left on this planet, and we had to drive forward regardless. To honor our king, we had to become royalty. We created in his image.

I rolled the window down. Damp, cold air pooled into the car and puddled at our feet as the light turned green.

Through the store's plate glass, I was certain that I heard the muffled tones of The Dawn Ego EP playing as we pulled away. Paul hadn't picked his magazine back up, but nodded his head to the light thumping of John's bass drum.

Chapter 8

Friday.

We had just finished unpacking the white, windowless van beside the café outside the loading door. I realized there was one more box that I needed to take in before John moved the van that John's uncle used for his Vietnamese restaurant.

The last box. Thirty more copies of the EP. Five bucks each. Two hundred stickers to be freely distributed by Paul and Jenny as the audience left.

It was a brisk night, and the weather was changing for the better. Buds hung on the trees along the sidewalk, and the moon was bright and sharp with atmospherically clear clouds trailing across it. In the west, a pitch darkness trailed like a line across the night sky. Above one half hung cumulonimbus clouds lazily dragging over the heavenly orb. The other half was a cloak of nothingness seeping into clarity surrounded by cutouts of a billion brilliant stars.

I walked to the door and lay the box on the floor next to some microphone stands and cables. John appeared in the doorway.

"Where do you think I should park it?" He asked.

"Want to bring it around the corner off of the street so everyone can park?"

"Makes sense to me." John got in the van and drove away. The exhaust hung in the crisp air for a moment before dissipating.

I turned back into the cafe and pulled the heavy steel door behind me. A whoosh of cold air curled around me before being replaced by an intimate warmth.

We were assigned a spot near the back door. To the immediate left was a hallway with bathrooms and a second entrance to the supply storage area and presumably the office. The performance space was straight ahead in the deepest corner of the cafe, a rudimentary stage made from some old pallets. We put a rug down, and put an overhead projector that shone a transparency of the band's name and our presidential ouroboros on the wall.

John had already set up his drums, and Steve was arranging the amplifiers and microphones just so. I taped the set lists to the monitors. Everything was in its place, and the band was enjoying cappuccinos and buttoning up the final arrangement of our equipment. In an hour, we would be performing our first show.

The past week was a blur of working, studying, making new posters, hanging them around town, and doing all manner of preparation for this first night. The easiest part of the week was my school work, the best was rehearsing, and the warmest was Jenny.

The two nights I worked at Kinkos were relatively easy. After some simple training, I was finally taking care of customers on my own the second night. On my first night I got several Oxford shirts, and they loaded me up on tchotchkes. They gave me a nice pen and a keychain with a triangle work-life-passion spinner on it. The keychain was a weird gift for your first night.

Of course, my favorite part of the job was the discount. In the span of the past week, I designed and cut three different poster styles based on the original designs to promote the show. Nonsequiturs such as "new," "grunge," "coffee and rock," "processed cheesefood product," puzzled the eye. Most importantly, they had a time, a venue, and "all new house band" emblazoned across them. I was able to print six hundred posters on a variety of colored cardstocks for six dollars after my employee discount, and an added "he might be able to tell there's more in this stack, but won't say anything about the number I gave him" discount.

Each member of the band destroyed the school, the community, stores, doctor's offices, gyms, and bathrooms with our posters. Twin Falls sunk under a colored snowfall of excitement, color, and immediacy. Cars had them under their windshields, supermarkets had them wrapped around automatic doors, and the library bulletin boards were sick with them. It was as if Twin Falls was a dragonian and serpentine ouroboros in its own right, rainbow scales fresh from molting under the new guidance of rock and roll.

So here we were. It was our first show and we were ready. It was all going to be a surprise, unique in the world.

John returned and made final adjustments to his drum kit.

"How are we looking?" Paul asked. "Todd, John, can I get you a drink? You guys didn't get anything yet."

"I think I'll wait until we're done. Nerves." John responded similarly.

"No problem. So we're about fifteen minutes out, and I think I would like to introduce you once I sell some things and then invite you on stage. What do you have left to do before I unlock the door?"

"Sound check, I guess, just to make sure it is the right levels. Some final tuning."

"Great. Just head on out back when you are done and I'll open up."

My heart began to feel the weight of actually starting this thing. I picked up my guitar, and my hand felt sweaty against the polished enamel and the silky strings. I was nervous.

I clicked the amplifier on. The light warmed on and the hum began to expose me to the room as it bloomed. Steve and

Kurt stood at the ready, and I could hear the ka-klack of John picking up his sticks off his snare drum.

We began to play our first song, adjusting the sound for the space as we went. The bass bounced the little room from floor to ceiling, and was greased with the polish of the guitar's treble. The mirrors shook and vibrated with excitement and purity. It was a natural cohesion of sound and space, and we hammered down the song as if it was our duty to do it all along. Everything was perfect before we even finished the song.

We put our instruments down and walked into the little back room. Stock surrounded us, floor to ceiling. Foam cups, bags of beans, straws, and stock boxes climbed to the ceiling, and we found ourselves in a forest of industrial foodservice.

Up the hall we heard the ca-chunk of Paul releasing the bolt on the front door, and a bajingle with every opening of the door.

"I call this first meeting of the band of the next decade," I began with a sniffle and a nod. They were modest men of little words, but incredible talent. They smiled and acknowledged me, and it was a moment of revelation and acceptance of our fates together.

Bajingle.

"Let's talk about tonight. We have our set lists, and everything is all set. What are we forgetting?"

"What do we do after the first half hour?" Steve 'The Practical' had a point.

"Right. Well, we haven't really gone much farther than

that, have we? Five songs, about three to five minutes each. Consensus, gentlemen: what do you think we should do?"

Bajingle-Bajingle.

The whoosh of the espresso machine.

"I think we should jam," Kurt interjected. "In between. We've done well with that." The man said little, but it was always a gem of wisdom.

I looked at John and Steve, and they nodded in agreement.

Bajingle.

"John, when we finish a song, start...something jazzy, four-four, and we will come in? Do you want to change key each song, or keep to the same?"

"I call sticking to C or E," Steve began. "Most of our songs are there anyway, and it would transition well."

"Good call. And maybe a little intermission in the middle or so? Go no longer than seven minutes of that, and move to a real song?"

"Sure," Steve continued, "and let's alternate, C, E, C, E, C."

Bajingle.

Kurt seemed happy.

"Kurt?" Steve wanted to check.

"You guys are on rhythm and bass, so I will just do what makes sense."

Bajingle.

"Perfect."

Bajingle. Wooshshshshshhhh. Spa-clink.

"Anything else?" I scanned. No one seemed to have any comment - bajingle - and I wanted to commemorate the night with a rallying battle cry.

In one of my classes we read the speech from Henry IV about Saint Crispin and coming back with scars and talking about the triumph of the day even though the battle was dire and it was impossible to win the war. We were going into this show with absolutely nothing - bajingle - and like Hal I was leading this small band of brothers to the front with little more than an idea and a few songs.

This wasn't Shakespeare. This wasn't war.

Just start, already.

"We are here tonight to do something new. We are here to make a community stronger, to make our bond stronger, to make a masterpiece of music and sound (bajingle) and a bond of determination. We will rouse the saints of goodly notes (bajingle) and trumpet them on high to our small audience. We will be their sound-gods, carrying the armies of the muses to the forefront of our little cafe in the middle of Twin Falls Idaho, and purchase their hearts and minds to follow us. They will revel in us.

"We are going to carry the children of Twin Falls to their musical apex, assisting them to be the notes, and march to our rhythms like the little cherub rats of Hamelin following their note-driven Piper away."

Where was I getting this stuff? The espresso maker

'whoowoowooshed' in response.

"So tonight, we drink in our music and our successes. We focus on what we are and what energies we have. We focus on everything we want to be because of everything that has come before us and drives through us. We do it tonight because Cobain can't."

From down the hall we heard a change in the atmosphere. The silence was immediately apparent.

"Ladies and gentlemen," Paul began, "Welcome to the Caffeine Machine's first show in what we hope will be a new perio...." I tried to stop paying attention so I could finish my speech.

"We will be going out there in a minute. But I wanted to just-"

"...and here they are, for the first time at-"

"I wanted to say, thank you for going on this journey with me. Let's go out and have some fun and really make some magic." I put my hand in the middle, and then Kurt, and then Steve, and then John. "We are-"

"Ladies and gentlemen,"

Paul, John, Steve, Kurt, and I said it together.

"The Dawn Ego."

We left the stockroom and turned down the hall. At the end of the hallway, a face appeared. Two faces. Three, layered. As the threshold approached and widened with perspective of the room, it became apparent.

We dove into a sea of bodies. Bodies on the floor sitting

cross-legged, bodies against the wall standing, bodies layered on bodies. There were people from school - Jenny was front and center - but there were few I could recognize individually in this sea. The people were amass amid the scent of coffee and cinnamon, sweet cream and nutmeg. Was that hundreds of bodies? And fabric? And cologne?!

They clapped, cheered, and we walked awash in the cotton of applause. We entered this storm. There must have been seventy-five people in that tiny room. More?

The windows of the restaurant dripped with condensation, foggy like a late night drive. It was incredible. They were all here for us.

John sat at his drums, and began a beat as we pulled our guitars over our heads.

The hum of the amplifiers.

I turned to Kurt and nodded. He nodded.

I turned to Steve and nodded. He nodded.

I turned to John and nodded. He nodded.

The hi-hats counted out. One, I turned back to the audience. Two, I approached the mic. Three, I positioned my hand and raised my pick. A silent four, and I looked up.

My hand dropped through space.

The pick made contact.

Chapter 9

The sounds crept up through the black universe and down through the electric blue of existence. The notes communicated our souls into the minds of our audience, and we had control over them as they dematerialized before us, and regenerated through John's tribal beat.

They bowed down before us in utter cohesion, kowtowing gracefully to submit to our desires and our sound. We had them through the intensity of our performance, a twist of a head, a bend of a note, a foot on a monitor, and a wink from behind a microphone. We were terribly true to our audience. We kept them rapt with attention and devotion to our sound waves for an hour and a half.

The silence of the short intermission was broken by the trade of cash for merchandise and drinks at the counter, and we appreciated Paul's 'thank yous' and incessant hawking of our EP with every sale.

Our coven of admirers worshipped and bowed to the sounds of our guitars. It was our truth. We were the spark to the conflagration, huddled toward the middle of a room surrounded by frosty-needled condensed glass. A mean sizzle of caffeinated meat in our foreground just beyond the microphones stood receiving electrons firing from our heads. We all, audience and band, beamed with an electronic fuzz and narcotic buzz.

This was now, this was here, and this was everything.

We walked the tightrope of artistic endeavor, and as we played the final chords of the show, our heartbeats slowed. Our audience's hearts slowed. Everyone was in synchronization with the spinning charm of our universe. We wound the charm down with our eyes closed, adjusted to the darkness behind our eyelids, and we pushed this through our audience.

We were all...right there.

The final G, and the

tss

      tss

         tss

            tss

               tss

                  tss

                     tss

                        tss

tss of the ride cymbal, and the cymbal and the bass faded,
and faded,

and faded,

and was tiny as a mouse before we breathed in, breathed out, and relaxed. The crowd hung, and then a roar of applause cantered through the small space in every cubic inch of air. Applause, a reciprocal gesture of appreciation for our art and our performance, echoed back among us.

"On drums, Johnny X," and a roar as he stood and a quick bow. "On bass guitar Steve Harvester," bow, cheer, "Kurt Lobel on lead guitar," nod, cheer, "And I am Todd Keefe and we are The Dawn Ego." One final resounding cheer. We put our instruments down, and played the mix tape in the deck hooked up to the PA system for the post-show music.

The energy in the room was enthusiastic and beautiful as friends and family of the band surrounded each member. The virtual line separating the performance space from the audience blurred to nothing. Waves of bodies congregated around each of them like networked nodes thirsty for energy.

Jenny sprouted up and swept her arms around me in an enthusiastic and warm embrace. Her strength and support was just as evident in her hug as her endearing lust and pride. Jenny put her lips next to my ear as a whizzle of chatter filled the room.

"You were incredible!" She whispered. She kissed my cheek, and continued up my jawline, "and hot!" She bit my earlobe and a tingle of warmth shot up my legs.

"What do you really think of it, since you've seen us in practice?"

She pulled back for her frank review.

"Obviously, you guys were ready for an audience. I know you were nervous...not for the performing part but for the songs. You really pulled it off."

"We did?"

"You did. Did you see Mr. Lloyd is here?"

"Who?"

"English? He came. He was beaming the whole show!"

"I didn't know he even cared - I don't mind being wrong."

"Yeah. He left right away, but you could tell he really liked it. Todd, your English teacher came to your show!"

Jenny's attention turned to Paul as he walked up.

"That was great," he said, sticking his hand out. I enjoyed it a lot."

"I am glad you did. Did you make a lot of money?"

"Best night I've ever had, as a matter of fact. You guys are welcome to come back whenever you want - next week, or two weeks to get a break, and in the meantime if you have any friends who want to come and do a show... whatever!"

"Thanks, Paul. I'll talk to the guys."

Paul nodded with a smile and watched the patrons slowly filter out.

"Take your time packing up. I still have cleaning and stuff to do, anyway." He turned and walked behind the counter.

"I suppose we should get out of his hair. Want to lend a

hand?" Jenny nodded with her hands clasped in front of her, her breasts smooching out in her sweater. She looked amazing.

We began unhooking and crating cables, moving boxes and amps toward the mental door, organizing, securing, and making sure everything was in its right place.

John ran out of the cafe to fetch the van and pull it up beside the building. Once the band had finished with their goodbyes and we were the only people left in the building, it was only a matter of a half hour before the van was packed and ready to go.

I led the way back in, checking the floor for scratches, trash, or any other nuisance we may have caused. Nothing was left - we were spotless and left not a trace that we had ever been there.

I approached the counter with the guys, and Paul was doing final wipe-downs of the counters and the cash register.

"Paul, we wanted to thank you again for all of your great work and being such a good host for us tonight."

"Thank you, gentlemen!" He held his hand out for us, and we each took a turn shaking it. "I would love to have you back again real soon. You are exactly what we need - not just my store, but to get the community out and engaged. This is exactly what I had in mind for these little shows. I would be totally willing to have anyone like you here at any time - so tell your friends or any other local bands. You did a smashing job with everything. Thank you."

"I'll give you a call when we figure out what we want to do

next," I replied, "but we absolutely want to be back soon."

We turned to leave.

"Wait!" Paul shimmied around the counter to meet us on the way out. He had the merchandise box in his hands.

"Oh, I almost forgot to grab those."

"These?" He opened the box, and it was empty, save for a pile of cash. "Sold them all. Almost a hundred and fifty bucks. Want me to get rid of the box?"

I reached in and picked up the wad of cash. I felt the band's eyes burning over my shoulders at the power of this money - money fairly earned doing what we loved. The power of asking, and exchanging our tapes for money. It was incredible. We earned this with art. Somehow, it was heavy in my hands, and it felt dirty, hot, stinging, and powerful to behold.

I was stricken as deeply as the other men.

"Thank you."

"You're welcome - you should have made more, I had to turn some people away."

"Amazing."

"Good night, boys."

And a smattering of 'good nights' and we were out the door standing next to the van with a wad of money. Me, Jenny, Johnny, Kurt, and Steve.

We were speechless.

Johnny was the first one to speak.

"BB's?"

Speechless, we piled in the van, and Jenny ran over to her

car parked across the street.

The seating situation in the van was not ideal with only two legally seat-belted passengers. Kurt and I bounced on the equipment in the back of the van, our backbones bruised and our skulls rattled. When not trying to remain upright, we tried to prevent the heavy and expensive equipment from landing on us.

We always managed to make it in one piece.

BB's Breakfast and Biscuits was on the edge of town, far from everything, but it was one of the few twenty-four hour joints. Kurt and I clambered out of the back of the van, and Jenny met us at the door. It was eleven thirty, and the five of us walked in to the late-seventies halogen oasis like we owned the night.

We were masters of the domain with a hundred and fifty bucks to spend on anything we wanted, like being the richest people in the room. We were invincible.

We were the only people in the room.

We were brought to a round booth, each given a seventeen page laminated menu. We studied with our stomachs on our eyes, lapping up the coronary-inducing fare that didn't matter at eighteen years old. This was our moment.

I ordered a patty melt sandwich on rye that came with a little cup of coleslaw and a pile of fries. I ordered an extra side of fries, because even though Jenny was getting the grilled chicken salad plate, she would always eat my fries if I didn't order extras.

"I mean, you were standing with your legs apart, total

rock stance, and you didn't give a shit, man!" Kurt was giving Steve a hard time about his stage presence after we ordered.

"That was badass," I interjected.

"I just, what?" Steve questioned.

"It's not like you, man, that's all. The holy spirit of rock entered you and saved you," Kurt said.

"I want to thank you guys," I said. "This couldn't have gone any better, and I wasn't sure we were going to be ready. This was really awesome. I saw nothing wrong with our performance tonight. Really."

"He was freaking out." Jenny felt the need to clarify my pre-show jitters.

"Regardless of that, we gave it a lot, made some money, made a professional contact. It was awesome."

"What do you think about us going back?" Steve asked.

"It's a great idea - we could be The Caffeine Machine house band or something. Hell, we could practically hold practice there every week. If you count our jams in between songs, we basically had practice tonight, right?" Everyone chuckled. "The only thing that I think is a bit rough is being able to keep up that momentum about getting people to come out."

"True." Kurt changed tone, "Which makes me want to say, and I can't speak for everyone, but I think you should keep the money since you invested the time and money on the tapes and posters and got that gig. It just seems right."

"Yes," John and Steve replied simultaneously.

"Come on, though, really?"

"Just reinvest it in us or something. Use it to make more tapes and things."

"That is reasonable. But dinner tonight is on The Dawn Ego."

"You bet your ass, it is," John replied.

And the food came and we ate, jokingly revisiting the moments, enthusiasms, and successes of the past twenty-four hours.

When we finished, our plates were those of soldiers after the wars. We had shoveled food down our gullets to make up for the famine of the battlefield, and the stoneware was bone-clean.

Ours was the battlefield of pop; the battlefield of taste, and rock, and everything that is good in this world against the forces of evil. It was the battlefield of corporate greed and tasteless sheep-feed they stuffed down our throats on the radio and television and the department stores selling boxes and boxes of faded dreams. In the face of living, the machine shoves these broken dreams of youth in big boxes at us for the money we willingly pump into their pockets. Nightmares. Once you bought the dream, it faded quicker than your years.

I enthusiastically paid the waitress, and we clambered back to the van. Jenny stood on tiptoe next to me and whispered in my ear, "see you in bed," and walked back to her car. I felt carnal looking at her ass. It shook under a flannel shirt as she stepped into her driver's seat.

It was nearing one in the morning. Our energy, enthusiasm, youth, and rock and roll remained coursing through our veins. I would never sleep again.

Steve and I piled into the back of the van this time, and Johnny drove with Kurt up front. Everyone was parked at my house, and we would quickly unload the van as soon as we got home before everyone left to go back to their houses.

He started up the van and began to pull out. The tape deck continued to play bootleg college radio station playlists featuring incredible bands whose sounds shook the foundations of regular radio. One moment, the young announcer mentioned Sonic Youth, and in the next breath he presented a song by Guided By Voices - or at least it seemed like a snippet of a song only moments long - incredible, hard, rocking, low-fi power grunge unlike anything I had ever heard.

"Who are these guys, John?"

"I have no idea. Don't you love it though? I love these tapes I get."

"You should sell them or something. Or keep them. It is an incredible mix the college kids put together."

"I know."

We were driving on fifty, and ahead a pair of bounding high-beamed headlights bounced and bounced and bounced toward us in the opposite direction as we neared the bridge over Snake River Canyon.

The song on the cassette stopped halfway through, and the hiss of the end of the tape, and a ka-chuck, and the hiss of the beginning.

"They've got to put a CD player in this, soon," John said

as we drove over the bridge.

Snake River, I thought.

The approaching vehicle was a Bronco, bouncing on an overcharged suspension. It seemed hastily attached, raising the truck almost too high for its bizarrely small wheels, and the headlights grew in the frame of our windshield.

Snake River.

The bronco moved quickly like a train toward us, staggering on the suspension, faster, faster.

"Snake river," I said, "We were almost 'Ouroboros.'"

Lights. Brilliant lights, before,

the truck slammed into us,

and everything seemed willing to be studied in a moment.

I saw the grey form of the driver, as if he wasn't there but was a shadow. The sound of the impact, spa-crackle of glass, slowly, and the front fender of the Bronco travelled into the corner frame of the truck, John's head moved forward with momentum but stopped only by the arriving bumper smashing through the frame and the glass and his head travelling backward again with the glint of chrome. Steve continued forward, and forward, and forward, horizontally swimming like a pencil through the air, and straight through the broken windshield, and he was gone. I didn't move, stuck behind some the amplifiers jamming into John's seat. I was pinched like a vise somewhere.

The Bronco heaved above us like a hinge as we began

screeching sideways in a reciprocal opposing force. It was natural. The physics of it all seemed to make sense in the calm, slow motion study. My appreciation was beautifully magnified in this trance of time's elongated terror.

Kurt, seat belted, jerked to the left and now down, rag-dolled into the seat and up, and down again as if he were in one place and the van moved around him. My forty pound fender amplifier finally bounded forward with kinetic energy and slammed into the dashboard.

There was a hiccup of steel, and I noticed the amplifier remained suspended in the air rather than falling to the floor. Kurt's arms involuntarily hung in the air as if he were on a roller coaster. The van had begun to spin, and I realized through the windshield that the horizon was all messed up. The headlights, still functioning, reflected on pavement, and then steel guardrail, and then dark spring-night sky, and then nothing, and then trees, and then the underside of a bridge. My rising organs choked me, and my muscles tensed in reaction to my dire situation.

Wind. It picked up. It whooshed.

Then an impact-clap as we hit the brick wall of water on the bottom of the van, and I watched the amplifier come down hard on the floor just as I felt gravity pull and pull and pull and pull and pull down down down down down, folding me down like a piece of flat paper and my face flatte-

Chapter 10

Wet.

Cold wet like piss and stink of mudflat.

A groggle of a winch, blink.

A ringing in my ears, stuck and clammy mouth of mud.

Choke.

Ouroboros.

Lights. I was standing and there were lights, flashy blue and white. Sparkle-white and red. Red white and blue. A dream. American dream. Filled to the topful o'cherry pie fireworks.

I was standing against a...what?

This is a fire truck, and there is a light in my eyes. This is a light shining in my eyes to check my eyes.

"How are you doing, pal?"

"Ouroboros."

"Oh yeah? Not really big on my Greeks or anything, but... What is your name?"

"Dawn Ego."

"John, what, my man?"

"Todd." My legs were killing me, My back was killing me. Pins and needles. I didn't know why he insisted I stand against this stiff truck. Why after talking with me for a few minutes, he was shining the lights back and forth and back and forth and back and forth, and as soon as one of my eyes were used to the dark, he moved it back over to the other eye and I couldn't see a thing. My eyes were opening, closing in concert.

In cement.

"Oh, Todd, okay."

"Todd."

"Stay with me, Todd."

"I'm right here."

"You're doing great, now. What year is it?"

"1994."

"Who is president?"

"Nixon."

"Kid, Nixon was barely around when I was born."

"Nixon was the Ouroboros. I meant Clinton."

"You got it, bud." He stopped it with the flashlight. The crystalline spots hung. "Breathe."

"Yeah." What?

"Good, breathing is getting back to normal. Vitals."

"Yeah." My eyes adjusted and I still couldn't see his face, the lights in my periphery contributing to a blinding ocular magic trick.

Steve walked over. I could barely make him out.

"Hey! Boy."

"What happened?"

"Accident."

"Obviously."

"I'm fine, I was just over there." A strange glitch of black and then the light of the flashlight again, and Steve continued. "Sometimes, I have a real problem with chili. Like real bad. Copper penny bad."

"Yeah." It made no sense, but I couldn't tell what was happening.

"Anyway, I was over there. Seemed like I missed the worst of it. Glad I got out of there! John and that van with no seatbelts in the back. Boy. Copper penny luck, I can tell you. Heads or tails, and a staple in your bellbottom."

I was too embarrassed to ask what he was talking about, because it was probably my head. Then, I remembered the bumper to the Bronco slamming through the corner of the van into John's face.

"What about John?"

"John? He's ok, look."

My perspective of vision altered. Probably my head, again, but I saw him lying on a stretcher with a bandage around his entire head like the invisible man. His tee shirt and jeans were clean except for sparkly glass pieces sprinkled on him like the fake snow in Christmas mall displays. He held a thumb up from his laying position like an injured daredevil. He looked at me through the gauze, somehow, and somehow I was watching above him? Or next to him? No, I was watching him be wheeled and his stretcher tucked into the ambulance.

"Kurt?"

"He already left."

"Oh. Is he... ok?"

"Oh, sure, you know Kurt ˗ he is always okay. Doesn't bother anyone with anything. White bread and molasses."

What?

"What about the guy in the van?"

"Dead. Drunk, dead, and in the grave, the drunk."

"That's terrible."

"What'd you expect?"

"Well... I didn't expect you to talk like that."

"He shouldn't have been hopping around on the moon scooter tires." I knew nothing about cars.

"Even so, we should have respect, because we're okay."

"Yes."

"All that gear and the fan and this man, just a terrible, terrible."

"All insured, thanks to uncle Xiong."

"Uncle Xiong?"

"Johnny's uncle Xiong, of the Vietnamese."

"...restaurant?"

"Yeah."

It was astonishing, what a night.

I patted about myself and everything was awake and functioning. I was here. This would be the story of the ages - one for our children or grandchildren. The night Papa was a rock star, the night Dad got a second chance. The night to begin all nights.

I hovered above my bed, dreary and sick with fatigue. Or stood with a spacy waving back and forth.

I fell into bed, onto my back, and pulled deeper and deeper into slumber. Groanings in my spine, burned muscles, the sore sting of a night that began without event but turned into a station of relaxation. Relax. Relax.

The bedclothes surrounded me, and I sunk.

My mind was clearing and the smoke rose.

This was almost the end. This was the beginning.

I am not what I am.

Behind my eyes, a spinning, chewing, hungry Ouroboros. Scaly and splotchy skin. Chomp, slide-chomp, slide - open wide - chomp.

He massaged his tail down his throat.

Little

by little

by little.

Chapter 11

I awoke. The next morning was a strange atmosphere. I wanted orange juice. The room felt cast in an orange juice haze, somehow. I scratched my eyes and it cleared.

Jenny wasn't in my bed. I thought she would have stayed over.

My mind was afog.

The show. BB's.

I touched my head.

There was the accident.

I am here.

I rubbed my eyes again, and stars shot from the back like the flashlight of the... Firefighter?

Fire. No, accident.

I needed some breakfast, and a shower.

I walked downstairs. The familiar feel of gravity underfoot became the feeling of gravity endlessly pulling my body into the bottom of the van and into the ground. It was like in physics class when the teacher described that a table isn't supported by legs, the legs push the table up. Everything wants to fall. Gravity and time: how strange and disorienting.

The kitchen looked different, like explaining a dream, and it is your house, but it isn't really your house. Everything was there, though. I must have really hit my head hard. Everything was unfamiliar, building itself into existence.

I took down a bowl. I poured flakes in the bowl. I poured milk in the bowl. As it came out, it flashed inky white and coaly. Inky white and coal? Just white. Milkwhite black.

No, this was my mind. Where is my mind? A dream only because I was rehashing nothing. Reacclimating to reality. Reset.

Cereal. Flakes. Corn baked in an oven, with milk, and what I needed to begin to feel like myself once more. John Harvey Kellogg told me I would be having this and then a solid hour in the electrolysis tub and then - no. I am mashing this in with - ugh.

I brought the cereal to the kitchen table.

The kitchen table. A tablecloth that was themed in fall colors, even though fall was six months ago. It was ok. This is the way of things.

I put the first spoonful in my mouth, and the silverware tinked on my teeth. Flakes, still crisp, entered my mouth with jagged mountainous impacts on my hard palate roof as the cool and calming milk cascaded from the spoon. My jaw was open, but then slowly compacted the food creating a vacuum and smashing the mountains of processed corn under the heavy weight of the sea of milk.

The sound echoed in my skull.

It was a massacre of geologic proportions.

My eyes were closed, and I chewed and savored in the darkness.

The one thing about being in a near fatal car accident the night before and waking up in your own bed as if nothing had happened, was that there was a certain sense of this meal being the best thing I had ever tasted. These flakes of processed surplus corn smashed into baked flakes was somewhat of a religious experience when eaten in this fashion.

I was here. Here is the table and the tablecloth. There is a bowl in front of me. There is also a salt and pepper shaker. In this bowl there are flakes of reconstituted, baked corn that were purchased in a box at the supermarket, which I poured into this bowl and then soaked in milk. The milk broth added a savory, hearty element to the meal that would make it my high-energy input for the day. It was a supplement. A lubricant enriched with vitamins and minerals that helped the flakes slide down my gullet.

The spoon clinked on the bowl, and I continued to eat.

I ate, and acclimated myself to the sun's position along the horizon. I was secure and focused in my meal and in my mind.

That was it. Simply checked out. I hadn't entirely woken up yet, and perhaps my injuries weren't that bad. I got lucky. That gorge was deep, but apparently we hit it just right between the suspension on the van, the tires, and the water landing.

Incredible.

Why hadn't Jenny stayed over?

No matter. She probably waited in her car outside for half an hour, and not sure what was taking so long had turned around and left for home.

I finished my cereal and walked to the window, somehow expecting to see the van outside in the driveway. It wasn't

Hadn't I seen the sun?

I walked to the basement door, and stepped down the stairs to the cellar. All of our equipment sat in piles. There was a little water stain on the floor next to some of it, which was to be expected considering our watery plunge. I couldn't believe everything was here. I wondered if part of the salvage of the van included bringing the gear back to the house. But already? At least, I hope that John's uncle had insurance - it was a business van and the accident was the other guy's fault. Maybe the insurance company is why everything was taken care of right away.

I ran my fingers over my amplifier and the speaker cabinet. They were dry. My fingers pulled out some grass (marsh grass?) from the fabric in the front of the cabinet, but it didn't appear that it was there from the water. It was just, there.

I opened my guitar case which sat leaning against the

amplifier, expecting to find some gross injustice inside. Everything looked normal, snug, safe, and dry. The thing was surprisingly indestructible in the face of having landed in a river at the bottom of a drop that happened in a van with bodies and equipment in it.

My organic self was almost magically unharmed in this, but the discovery that my guitar and amp were safe was almost ludicrously generous. What had I done in a previous life to deserve this?

I returned upstairs, and mother was in the kitchen.

"Oh, Todd, I didn't hear you."

"I didn't hear you, either."

"How was the show?"

"Incredible. It couldn't have gone any better."

"I am so proud of you, Todd."

"Thanks."

"What time did you get in?"

"One, I think. There was a car accident and-"

"Oh, honey, are you okay?"

"Apparently." I didn't want to tell her about the Bronco, and falling off the highway into Snake River Canyon. I was safe, but even recounting it in that simple sentence 'falling off the highway into Snake River' would make it almost ridiculous that I was even standing here. Maybe it was.

"Was Jenny at the show?"

"Front and center."

"She is so good to you. Look outside! She is in the

driveway in her little red car!" The grammatical enthusiasm in her voice was strange.

I cocked my head, and slowly walked over to the window. Sure enough, her car was at the end of the driveway. Odd. I didn't notice it.

"I didn't know she was coming," I whispered to myself.

I walked out the front door and down the driveway to the side of the road where she was parked. I could only see the top of her head slumped down in the seat and pressed against the window like she was dead.

The window was rolled down a crack, and she was asleep.

I tappy-tapped on the window with my fingernails, and whispered 'Jenny,' through the small gap in the window.

Nothing.

I increased the tempo, the depth, the strength, the loudness, and repeated her name.

A stirring, her folded arms began to move as she craned her torso around. She looked up disoriented. Her head flipped in the direction of my knocks and she smiled drowsily.

"Hey babe," I said softly.

"Hi," she whispered through the glass. "You took a while to get home."

"I did."

"I was worried strong."

"I know. I'm here." Worried strong?

"Did you go home?"

"That's where we are. You're in your car outside my

house. We're talking through the glass."

She came to the realization of her circumstance. She licked in her mouth and cleaned around her teeth before reaching for the door handle.

I stepped back and the door swung open. She got out and stumbled a little before gaining her footing with the pull of morning gravity. A bump of hair was off to the side on her scalp, a lump cascading down in a bizarre fashion that compromised the appearance of her mental health. It wasn't often that her mortality and fragile nature was revealed, but when it was, it was something to behold.

"You're home now, and it's the morning?" She asked.

"I have no idea what time it is."

"I was in the car."

"Yeah, I didn't see you."

"You didn't see me sleeping outside of your house? In my car?"

"Well, no. I mean this morning." I was dancing around these lost twelve hours. "I am actually not entirely sure how I got home last night."

"What?"

"There was an accident. With the van."

"What?!"

"Yeah, a guy hit us and we wrecked it - say, were you here when we were unloading the equipment?"

"Probably," she said uncertain, her hand tossing in the air around her head.

"Me, neither - guess I was really tired." Tired, and the logistics of what was going on was incomprehensible.

The sun beat down on us. It was still chilly. The sun was bright. A bird flew by like a black laser.

"Well, are you going to invite me in?"

"Sorry, I guess I'm still kind of out of it. I hit my head, but they let me go."

We walked toward the house together.

"Last night was awesome, Todd."

"It was. In the last twenty-four hours I've had a crazy itch to write a bunch. Just song after song after song to have a sort of catalogue that I can pull from. I also had this crazy idea that I would put our music up on that America Online group thing I made for people who are fans to download whenever - they could just go on there and grab it. It doesn't make a lot of sense because of the time it would take to download them, but I am sure I could figure something out. I don't even know where to begin, so there's that."

"That sounds like a great idea to get people interested. Free doesn't always mean good, though."

"Neither does fifteen bucks."

"True."

We entered the house and went straight up to my room. I pressed play on the CD player, and a grunge rendition of Led Zeppelin's Heartbreaker began to play. Strange, I thought. I never heard it before.

"Are you going to write, or what? I can go grab a book

downstairs."

"That sounds excellent."

I organized my notebooks and tried to remember where I was. I felt like an amnesia patient with a bunch of unfinished, distant situations and projects. My notebooks were unfamiliar and disorienting. There were too many. I had that dream-feeling; this house was my house but not really my house.

The song wrapped up. Kurt Cobain explained the song, title, and band. It was a Nirvana cover. What CD was this? When had they done that? Where did this come from?

Jenny returned, but I remained buried in my notebooks. I moved my hand to the dial and turned the CD player down. I heard her get on the bed, and I remained on the floor at the foot of the bed with my notebooks and a pencil, writing.

My lyrical compositions swam in pages as messy poetry. All but a few of my songs started in this book.

My new words didn't seem to have any purpose beyond the overall focus being related to either a first show or a car crash. They were non sequiturs like "Snake River pulls me on / black reverend following down," and "the string sound of a car crash / a G Major mistake on a black night." I continued writing, "mother and a banjo, on death's line was a hobo." Where did this come from? Just like the new Led Zeppelin cover, these seemed familiar. Had Robert Plant also suffered some kind of blunt trauma as he wrote?

"You have to hear this," Jenny began, looking up from reading from her book. "Baudrillard, this guy, created the 'simulacrum' - well, sort of - and he writes about it all the time. He got it from Plato and some other writings in the fifteen-hundreds. Anyway, it's all about the real becoming real through our interpretation of real events. Of our interpretation of reality. The search for finding knowledge and total understanding of oneself and the universe is ultimately crap because it is all based on this human subjectivity. We are, in essence, delusional and crazy when we explore and try to find out more about a reality that only exists because of the individual us.

"I wonder what that says about art? Come here."

I turned myself around at the foot of the bed, and she was laying shirtless with the book on her stomach. Her breasts lay perfect on her chest.

"I have a story about last night, you know," Jenny continued, playfully facetious. "I came here hoping that I could completely go home with the lead singer of this band that I went to see. As his number one groupie and president of his fan club, I just had to bed him. According to this book, if I thought it, I am it."

She threw the book aside in the bed. She beckoned me to crawl on top of her. She continued as I crawled, "and since all human discovery and progress and everything else is a fruitless endeavor, and we are living in this simulation based on our consciousness and messed up concepts of what it means to be alive, that can only mean that there are two things that are certainly off limits to commentary like that. Two things that, regardless of the simulation and how it is portrayed, can completely derail the concept of the simulacrum and make it as ridiculous as it is in the context of these two things."

She began to kiss me. She was talking so very much in her breaths squeezed between the short moments our lips parted.

"Those things are?" I asked. Simulacrum would make a great band name.

"Art, obviously. It portrays and pokes fun of the avatars we are by creating an avatar of the avatar, thereby cutting it out of the fabric of existence to be on its own."

"Isn't mom home?" I asked in response to her hands.

"She left." How had she learned this?

"And?"

She pulled my shirt off, unbuttoned my pants, pulled them down with her feet, and I was hovering over her completely naked.

"This."

A carnal reality to set in motion my recovery and to remind me of my existence. It was beautiful and stunning and real. We were synchronized in the space, the simulacrum taken out of our orbit for only a momentary glimpse of eternity in a moment. It was entirely pure and energetic.

We stepped out of ourselves, by stepping into ourselves. Skin, flesh, the movement of sweat and the deconstruction of the idea of consciousness and words collided with the same energy as our bodies. We were silken and excited, needed each other more than anything in those moments. I felt myself penetrating her to the core of myself, and for hours I desperately tried my hardest to fuse myself with her with every thrust.

In the final moment, in an unusual, synchronous, exhausted climax, her orgasm arrived with a hiss.

Chapter 12

"But I am telling you, we're ready. If the only thing we need to worry about is a van, we can get that somehow or shove our equipment into our cars and hope for the best... whatever."

In the basement Steve outlined his plan for the Twin Falls music scene. The plan was to dominate it.

"Have you been feeling ok? You're acting-" I paused. What was this? "I don't know, your enthusiasm is awesome."

"I'm fine, man. Let's write something."

We rearranged the equipment back into the unity of our regular practice layout. I grabbed a bottle of glass cleaner, and we wiped everything down as we rearranged it, removing pieces of marsh grass, seaweed, and patches of caked mud. I plucked one wispy piece of marsh grass from the fabric of the speaker housing several times like a clown pulling a never-ending stream of hankies from his mouth.

It didn't seem real that our equipment wasn't a complete wash. Everything sparkled when we were done. It was more beautiful than before.

We plugged in each amplifier, checked each guitar, and examined the rims and wood of the drums for warping and damage. Nothing. It was as if the accident never happened. The tubes behind my amplifier were in perfect condition, even in the face of bounding around the van. Was it possible that I imagined the extent of the damage? Even the accident? I remembered Steve had been ejected from the van.

"Are you okay? What happened with you last night?" I asked as continued to arrange the room.

"I'm fine. Apparently the windshield slowed me down as it broke. We weren't going that fast to begin with, though. I just landed on the pavement and slid a little, I guess. I did hit my head and don't remember it all that much, but I woke up and it was fine. I don't know. Don't worry about it. Everyone is ok."

"Yeah." I didn't understand.

I ran upstairs to grab my notes, and mother intercepted me in the kitchen. I don't know why I didn't expect to see her, and I felt my dream defamiliarization return in the kitchen that wasn't really our kitchen in the house that wasn't really our house, but was. The floor tilted under me, and her face was foggy around the frame of her jawline and indirect parsing of the scene. I had a hard time focusing on her.

"Hi, honey, how was your show last night?"

"You already asked me that..." She waited for an answer. "It went great. There were a lot of people."

"That's wonderful," her face was fuzzy and indistinct, even though all the pieces were there. I couldn't directly see an eye or nose or mouth. She was peripheral. "I know Stevie is here," (Stevie?). "There's a message on the answering machine for you."

"Thanks."

I walked into the dining room to the little white box with the blinking blue button on it, and pressed the button.

"MESSAGE SENT...TODAY,... AT... NINE-FORTY:" Two distinct voices on this old thing - the robotic voice of the machine, and the voice of the caller.

"Hi, this is Brenda over at Country Mortgag-" Skip button, beep, and the next recording began.

"MESSAGE SENT... TODAY,... AT... NINE-OH-THREE:"

"Hi, my name is Bruce Hirons. This is a completely unsolicited call, but I was at your show last night in Twin Falls and I got this phone number from Paul who gave me a flyer and your press kit. I was impressed with your performance and your EP. Why don't you give me a call back on my cell at..." and he finished with his number and to "call anytime." I quickly scrawled the number and 'Bruce Hirons' onto a piece of scrap paper.

I returned to the basement, and Steve was slapping around his bass, manipulating and bending the notes. He stopped to look up at me.

"Hey - I got a weird message on the phone upstairs about the show last night. Want to call back? Maybe we can do speakerphone?"

"Weird, like what? The accident?"

"No, the show. Maybe it's for the paper or something."

"Oh. Yeah."

We walked upstairs and into the living room where there was a separate phone we never used. It had a speakerphone. The only times that we ever attempted to use it was during holidays and family gatherings where we tried to send our blessings to a bunch of relatives all at once.

The phone was on a small end table, kitty corner to the sofa and love seat. I lifted the receiver, dialed the number, and pressed the speaker button. The ring sang through the small speaker.

"Bruce Hirons." He answered the phone with his name, a striking affirmative. A man was powerful when he answered without a particular 'hello' or 'good morning' or any modern phone etiquette. A response always felt difficult.

"Hi, Mr. Hirons, this is Todd Keefe from The Dawn Ego." I was struggling through this. I should have practiced it before calling. "My secretary (secretary?) left me a note that you called about the show last night. Just giving you a call back."

"Oh, yes, good. The Dawn Ego," he began. In the face of not knowing who this guy was, I thought I might look somewhat desperate and needy. I should have waited a few days to get back to him. At least a few days.

The business of art is nothing more than the art of relationships.

"...I called because I was impressed with the small set you performed last night. You were intimate and electric. I was really surprised. I was in town for my nephew's Bar Mitzvah, and I had nothing to do after the reception, and here I happen upon this little show in a little coffee shop in the middle of nowhere. I always try to check out the local scene wherever I go.

"Anyway, I bought your EP and I am going to take this back to the office in New York when I head back tonight. I would love for you guys to come and meet us and hang around the offices for the day. Maybe we can work something out."

Steve and I looked at each other, and didn't totally understand what he was saying.

"Okay, but... What?"

"Sorry, I work for Arista Records in New York. New acquisitions. Just a coincidence that I was in town and caught your show, but we're always looking for new artists and I really liked what I saw.

"What do you think?" Hirons asked.

Steve and I looked at each other in awe.

"Yes. Yes, absolutely."

"Excellent. Do you have a fax machine? I can send you paperwork that you can fill out about everyone in the band and we can get you guys some plane tickets and a hotel." I gave him the fax number for Kinkos. "Excellent. And this is Todd... Keefe, it says here, right? I'm heading back tonight and I will be in the office on Monday, so I probably won't get my secretary to send it until then if you don't mind waiting.

"Thanks for your time. I look forward to meeting the four of you. Have a great night."

"Thank you," I replied.

A click, followed by a few more clicks. Our stare was broken by the dial tone returning to the line. I hit the hook button, and the call ended. We sat wordless.

I broke the quiet. "I guess we need to tell the guys, right away."

"Perfect. Let's find Kurt and visit John in the hospital."

"We should do that, anyway. We haven't seen them since the accident. This will lighten their spirits considering we have good news!"

"Let's go now!"

We closed the house up, and got into Steve's car. Both cars, Mother's and Jenny's, were gone. I didn't even remember seeing them leave? Would they had stayed!

We pulled out. The sun shone through everything, as if everything solid was a gossamer transparency of golden summer. The roads were magically smooth, fresh pavement reflecting the afternoon sun through us and the telephone poles and the trees and the sparkling atmosphere bounced back off the seething black tar. The pzzzzzzz of singing locusts cut the air from their invisible hideaways.

We drove to the hospital first. The labyrinthine halls and turns opened up to rooms for patients in long term care. As we approached, gaggles of Vietnamese relatives kowtowed in the hall around his room, crying and turning beads over in their hands. A cloud of incense hung in flat sheets as we entered the room like a scene in Indiana Jones, and I wondered what all the crying and gnashing was about considering he seemed okay when I last saw him being carted off.

As we entered, he lay surrounded with candles and incense. There were candles in jars and some on their own with stalactites of wax dripping across and off the table, and there was something to say about the warm light feeling healthier than the oppressive halogen lights that hung above.

How did they get away with this? Maybe it was a religious thing. But the oxygen? Wasn't that the reason open flames weren't allowed?

John was in bed, surrounded by relatives in robes whispering soft prayers. He was wearing a silken red smoking jaket robe-type thing, matching pants, and leather slippers. Hospitalized Hugh Heffner, here, and his invisible-man-head-bandages remained a ghastly mask. His head was bandaged from the top of his crown, around and around and around, over his face, and conforming to the edges and reflections of his chin, and around and around his neck and down the front of the jacket. Circles of bandages, a Heffnerian cocoon, and no slits to see or breathe.

"Hello gentlemen," he began through the gauze and bandages. His voice was monotone, cool, and robotic.

"Hi." We both unsteadily acknowledged him.

His hand rose, and his head tilted. There was a string tied around it. He was an automaton.

"I am glad to see you both." The sound of his collected voice sounded unhampered by the bandages. It escaped clean and syllabic. "The doctors here have been treating me well and say I will be out of the hospital soon.

"I am lucky that I have great care and the support of my family." His hand swept across the people knelt beside him as he spoke like a king presenting his subjects. The people hadn't even acknowledged our presence. It was as if they were worshipping him as much as praying for him to get well.

"How much longer do you think you have?"

"A day, perhaps."

"What happened?"

"Nothing, but they just want to make sure. They have been worried about my face. They coated it in an anti-burn scar cream and stitched me up. They're just waiting for me to hatch."

That was a joke. Everything about the delivery of his words was off. How the hell was it so easy to hear him?

"Well, we're glad you are doing well," I continued. "We have some great news! We got a call on our answering machine and there was a guy from Arista Records at the show last night. He wants to meet us for a meeting in New York! They're flying us out and taking care of everything."

"That is interesting. I will likely stay here."

"Why? You won't be feeling well, so I get it, but-"

"I thought we were doing this as a hobby."

"We were. But the idea was that if we did well we'd see where it goes, right?"

"I will not be going. I will stay here. I am waiting for my college acceptances. I will get those and focus on going to college."

"Okay," Steve interjected, "but we figured that we'd be taking a year off from college and see where this goes. There isn't one way to do things, you know? We'll be fine."

"You don't understand." John's robotic, collected response was vexing. The gestures, the head tilting, all I could do was put another quarter in and watch him operate. He was imagineered, with a repetitive cycle of movements as a featured performer in The Carousel of Progress. He was jammed between generations, stuck repeating 'it's a bright big beautiful tomorrow,' over and over again in a horrific simulation of humanity. The oven kept exploding, and exploding, and exploding.

"I am waiting to hear back from MIT, Harvard, Oxbridge, and I will be going to whoever accepts me and moving on with my life. This band was a simulacrum of rock stardom. Our accident marked the end of my operation."

Oxbridge? Simulacrum? What was this?

"Well," Steve began, "we wish you luck. I know you'll get into MIT." Steve's words fed him more quarters.

"No, no, Steve, wait. John. John, last night you were fine and you really wanted to be a part of this and we had a great time. What happened?"

"I was hit in the face by a truck moving in the southbound

lane of the bridge over Snake River. I died, Todd, and then I was reborn." I wanted to punch the bandaged cocoon head, mechanically bounding back and forth through the same repetitive motions, over, and over, and over again. "I have a second chance. Everything is going to be okay."

Steve turned to me, and parroted, "everything is going to be okay." Was I the crazy one?

"Fine. Yes. Everybody's right." The weeping Vietnamese relatives remained with their heads bowed and their beads dancing in their hands across their mouths. This made no sense. Who let these fucking candles and incense in the hospital?

"Let us know if you change your mind," I continued. "This is all a good thing. I hope you get well. We can find another drummer, but we can't replace you."

"You're right."

I stood, shaking my head. John had stopped talking, and the robotic motions soundlessly continued.

"Bye John."

We turned to leave. The bodies of his relatives parted around us like the sea, and we the staff of Moses struck down into the sands on the shore. We were our exodus.

"So now to find Kurt, if he still wants to be in the band," reminding Steve of our mission. I realized I didn't normally know where to find Kurt.

We left the hospital and pulled out of the parking lot.

"And where is home for Kurt?" I asked. Steve shot me a look that communicated 'are you serious?' "What? I've never been there before. He's always come over to my place, or we've met him out."

"Down by the bridge," he replied, with an unspoken 'duh.'

We drove for five minutes and ended up by the high school. Steve directed me behind the building to a small bridge over a runoff stream that I had never noticed before.

We turned onto a service road, and down a vertical slope with such a steep diagonal grade that the car could barely hold on. The angle was nauseating. Two treads in the ditch worn away like scratches in the earth was the only indication it was even possible to drive on it. Steve took the wheel, and we zigzagged into the ditch. I covered my eyes as he steered; my perspective was a mess. He somehow folded into an impossible turn.

And we stopped. We were safe. It was so strange.

Steve got out and started walking under the bridge, and I followed. When we drove over it, the bridge looked three or four feet above the ditch. It's job was to bypass a little stream of water for drainage purposes. Once we were standing at the bottom, however, it towered almost ten feet above us.

The water trickled by in the mud.

I closed one eye, wracked with this impossible geometry of reality.

Was Kurt homeless?

A giant grate covered the pipe with weedy and swampen strings hanging from the horizontals. Steve walked me to the wall to the right to the pipe.

"Go ahead," he offered with a toss of his head, directing me to the wall beside the pipe.

Steve allowed me go first, to nowhere.

"Where?"

"There." No gestures. Nothing. Concrete wall.

"Where?"

He shook his head, frustrated, "there!" and pointed to a small hole in the wall that I hadn't bothered to notice. It was a square, deep, black hole as old as the concrete. Could I fit my head in, if I tried? If I was standing on tiptoe?

If I could, why would I?

"What am I supposed to do?"

Frustrated, he grabbed the back of my neck and walked me over to the hole like a child. The square was at face level, a little bit above my height, and he pushed my head into the cutout.

"Seriously? What are you doing?"

"Just go in, what are you waiting for? You're killing me! I'm dead!"

As he pushed my head forward, the hole surprisingly seemed wide enough for my shoulders, so I was able to wiggle in. He was right. I could fit. I wiggled in and wiggled in, and darkness began to envelop me as I pushed further in and the sunlight behind me was drowned out. It was a little tight, but not impossible.

It became somewhat difficult to breathe, musky mildew and stagnant basement air hung immobile. A little more wiggling and the hole turned from a square to a cylinder. Ahead, in what dim light there was, I saw a pair of sneakers snaking their way through with difficulty. Were they my sneakers? I wanted to bite them to hold on to them so I didn't lose my shoes. I wouldn't want to walk back out in the muddy marsh without my sneakers.

What?

Then, darkness.

I pushed harder and harder in, and it was tighter around my head and upper body as claustrophobia gripped me and I felt my head squeezing in deeper, unable to move. But then a pop, and cooler air freed me from my musky breathy moist lungbreath. My face was in a room, and the rest of my body remained in the tight grip of the tube like a chrysalis.

The tiny oblong room was fully furnished. My face felt like it took up an entire wall. There was a bookshelf, a little fire, and beautiful framed paintings that hung against the laws of physics along the walls that curved in a dome like the inside of an egg. There was a teapot with a steaming cup of oolong tea on a little side table, and a beautiful Victorian chair. Kurt sat in the chair, hiding behind a book. He was wearing an Offspring tee, jeans, Doc Martin's, and a flannel shirt tied around his waist. He was small, and my face was so big. He sat with his grunge posture in this big chair, his ass hanging off the seat and his shoulders barely clearing the back.

"Hello, friend," he greeted me. His voice was surprisingly normal, regardless of his appearance. This Beatrix Potter woodland den was perfect for him somehow, even though it was impossible. It was believable. This was where he lived. No wonder he never wanted me to see it.

"Hi, Kurt," I said. My voice echoed strangely in the little den. "What are you reading?"

He turned the book around and looked at the cover. Nothing was written on its leather binding.

"*The Screwtape Letters.*"

"Hmm," I responded. Never heard of it. I wanted to write it down - I would take a book he was devouring so intently very seriously. I wanted to look at it but I couldn't reach my hands.

A crack and a shaking came from the other side of the room, and a panting fell from the wall. Steve's big face appeared directly across from mine. We were the same size, at least. This was a miracle of dimension - our faces transforming the room into a cozy irony of dizzying gigantism and miniature scale.

"Hey, man," Steve said. "New painting? Sorry about that."

"It's okay."

"I never knew you lived here," I mentioned. That didn't make a whole lot of sense - I never knew he lived anywhere.

"Yeah, down the rabbit hole and into the hearts of millions." Neither did that.

"So," Steve began, "we are here to ask you about something, very easy." His eyes darted from me to Kurt, to me, to Kurt. "Todd, tell him."

"Yeah, so it turns out that a random record guy from Arista was at our show. They want us out in New York to meet with them and work on some deal. He is going to fax me Monday with some forms - but, basically we just want to know if you're in."

"Rad," and Kurt was back to his lachrymose, careless attitude. "I'm in."

"Excellent!" Steve was ecstatic. "There is one tiny little hiccup."

"Wait, how did this happen to begin with?" Kurt asked.

I started, "When I woke up, Mom told me that there was a message on the answering machine, and it was this guy. Steve had come over to work on some things. We called him back together."

The men, Kurt especially, were behaving uncharacteristically. Still, the momentum would be great for all of us.

"So, what is the hiccup?"

"Today we went to meet John at the hospital to tell him about the record deal, and he is still all bandaged up. He told us he was going to focus on college and that would be that. He's going to MIT."

"And?"

"And that's that."

"I thought we were going to take a year off from college. I mean, by 'we' I mean him because the rest of us didn't have any real plans."

"I know." Suddenly this felt like a real conversation. I had forgotten that I was a big face in a cubby-hole room next to a miniature crackling fire next to my miniature friend Kurt. It was a real discussion in the small, cozy cubby. "Listen, we can still do this. This is what we want. Let's see how long we can ride this train and make it work."

"Yeah," Steve echoed.

"Alright," Kurt added.

"We just need to find a new drummer. Piece of cake since we already recorded," Kurt reminded us.

"Well, we can go without him." Steve offered.

"Makes sense," I replied.

"Splendid," Kurt said. Splendid? "Give us a call when you have the trip figured out, and we can just go by your - who was it? Bruce? Bruce's plans."

Had I said his name?

"Okay. I will just call the both of you, and we will make it happen. We can find a drummer when we get back and just tell the label he couldn't make it."

"Saturday still?" Kurt asked.

"Yup."

"See you boys then," he replied, and picked his book back up and perfectly posed in the same fashion as when we arrived. Slouched, down, and transfixed. He was little statuary frozen in a Beatrix Potter diorama.

I shimmied my shoulders backward, and slithered back inch by inch. The hole of the little apartment got smaller and smaller, the aperture closed, my legs and my head could move a little, and my lungs finally filled.

I popped out of the hole, and the dark square in the concrete retreated from my vision as quickly as it had arrived.

"That was weird," I said to Steve, already standing behind me as he was before I went in.

"Give the guy a break," he replied.

I had to give the guy a break. For whatever reason that Kurt lived in a cubby under the bridge behind the high school, it was clear why we never went to visit him and he didn't have anyone over. It was a nice little place, though.

"At least we have everyone in besides John," Steve mentioned as we walked up to the car.

"Yeah."

"I honestly saw this coming a while back - he had been mentioning college the whole time. We could have been more cautious."

"I mean, did anyone honestly think that we would have a record executive offering us a deal the day after the coffee shop?"

"True."

We sat in the car. Steve was in the driver's seat. I had no idea how this car was going to scale the mud and rocks ahead of us to get us back to the road. Steve would navigate it fine considering he got us down here in the first place. The car started, and he gunned us forward. I covered my eyes again.

"What I don't get," I considered as Steve hauled the little car up the banks of the muddy, jagged, and impossible sluicey mound at incomprehensible angles, "is why he wouldn't humor us with wanting to do this. Especially since the record deal or whatever could potentially - perhaps easily - pay for college. I mean, what is MIT, twenty thousand a year or something? If they gave us a deal that left us each eighty-k at the end of it all, he would be all set. I might not know what I am talking about, but a record deal at three hundred grand seems like a small one."

We returned to the road toward my house.

"I don't have any idea how it works."

"Okay, but if we are talking about it costing the same to the record company as an expensive house, that seems to make sense to me."

"I see your point, but he already made his decision."

"I'm just saying."

We pulled up to my house, and Steve waited until I got out.

"So, I'll give you and Kurt a call and let you know what that paperwork looks like when I go to work at the copy shop Monday afternoon. What is the soonest you can pack up and be ready to go if he wants us in New York right away?"

"Whenever you think. I'm sure Kurt is the same."

"Good. I'll give you a call Monday when I get out and we can work out the logistics from there... I had a great day with you, man. I really like this new enthusiasm and passion you have for the band."

"This is all going to come together."

I opened the car door and walked toward the house. As I walked up the drive, my pacing slowed. The house seemed to move further away as I walked.

The sky seemed to darken into dusk, and I feel like I fell or dove into something and the world folded over into itself as I nuzzled in bed next to Jenny.

...Who was there?

...It was all very bizarre.

Chapter 13

"I think we should have a game plan going into this so that we don't get screwed over," I said as we drove down the packed boulevard. Buildings sandwiched us in shade as the car darted along. The structures were so immense that their heads swam in a cloud of fog.

The congestion on Broadway was palpable on the hazy, smoky dirt-milk of a Thursday morning. The three of us sat in the back of a cab that smelled like curry yellow cheese curl dust. A strange fear crept up me as I watched people in various stages of depressive horror wandering in front of Sbarro, Roy Rogers, and down and out pornographic establishments.

Our yellow Crown Victoria picked us up outside JFK Airport only four days after our performance at Paul's coffee shop. Our driver held a sign that said "Dawn Ego" on it. We had no trouble on our way except for the guy that thought we cut the cab line and called us assholes. He was right - we were a bunch of assholes. But we didn't cut.

The fog descended around the cab as we waited at a stop light. The veil of milky white cloud ebbed over the cab like the slow motion pour of a water tub a winning team pours over their coach. The waves and curls of fog devoured a dollar porn theater and then the trenched black man passing with a bottle in a paper bag. The mist devoured our cab, covering every window as if we were travelling down the Congo, the screams of car horns and 'fuck yous' hitting us from every unseen angle.

"I don't really know what to expect." Steve spoke with the genuine naivety that we all felt.

"Let's go in with some sort of solid plan of the least of our expectations. But we start big. Let them work for it. That way, even if they their expectations are different, we don't compromise lower than we deserve."

The thick blanket of fog still surrounded the vehicle, and yet the cab moved on. It was difficult to parse where we were going and how we were getting there. Perhaps this was normal? The cab driver seemed fearless, like this was just a normal day on the job. It felt like we were falling.

"So what are we going to demand?" Kurt asked.

"Let's make a list. What is it we want? I want to pay for college when this is over, just as my backup, so we should shoot for a base amount. What would you say to at least twenty thousand each year of our contract as well as the rights to a percentage of sales of CDs and merchandise?"

"For three, or for four of us?" Steve made sense - we needed a specific number.

"Four, obviously."

"So that is," he looked into his skull, "a hundred and sixty thousand dollars with a two year contract. We actually would just end up with eighty-k each year of the contract."

"That a good minimum?" I needed validation.

They nodded.

"I think we should also get equipment sponsorship, recording and tour related expenses, and whatever else so those numbers stay. I think no matter what, touring, food, equipment, and recording are part of our contract - that way our take home pay doesn't get eaten up when they want us to foot the bill for their expenses by being sneaky."

"Perfect," Steve responded.

"The way I see it," I continued, "is that all of this stuff they might want to work into the contract they will already own, or can sell as assets when our contract is over. So while we wouldn't get to keep it, they would get to reclaim some of that money and it is essentially their stuff anyway. They probably have full time drivers and things like that on the payroll for tours anyway, and all the other stuff in garages, and hangars, or whatever."

The cab stopped, and the waterfog lifted. It drained from a heavenly bathtub in a spiral above our heads.

"Here you go," the cab driver said, "Arista Records,

Midtown West."

We piled out in front of a big sloping building in the vertically oppressive city. This was decidedly not Twin Falls, and we were infected with the people and the excitement and the energy of our potential. This was it.

We entered. The concierge greeted us at the desk. As Steve talked to him, Kurt hit me and I spun around.

"Whoa!" He was pointing to a determined man with long hair walking out of the building.

"What?"

"Dude that was Brad Roberts."

"Who?"

"Crash Test Dummies, man!"

"Oh."

"Guys," Steve beckoned us to the elevator.

The elevator doors closed. Gravity pulled us into the floor, and my ears popped before the tug levelled off. The car began to tumble and shake. The horizon changed, and we had to step on the walls of the elevator to stay upright as it tumbled up the shaft. My eyeball muscles tensed, confused as the lights flickered, and then we were scrambling to gain footing on the ceiling (now the floor) and avoid the emergency door, and back around to the side again. I tripped on the wall bars, but gained my footing. We bounced off one another with our arms out to gain some leaning purchase on a wall or one another as the elevator slowed to a stop and was upright again.

Bing! The doors parted. I felt bad for the dusty foot marks

we left on the walls and ceiling. That didn't leave a very good first impression.

We were greeted with a mod-design waiting room of steel and blue fixtures, and *Arista* in brushed steel above the reception desk. Televisions flickered with music videos, and the area was clean and smelled like new car. Music we hadn't heard before played over the speakers in the ceiling. It was hip, saucy, and sharp.

We introduced ourselves to the receptionist.

"The Dawn Ego. Right this way."

She brought us through a automatic lock door she shut off with a buzzer, and through an open office area with low-walled cubicles. She turned at a room filled floor to ceiling with snacks, and large coolers with soda, water, and booze.

"Can I offer you anything?" She presented her hand to the doorway. We walked in and ransacked the junk food and soda, and she waited patiently. Kurt ate three bags of Doritos, almost including the bag, and a few Slim Jims, and swallowed, swallowed, swallowed it all down. He practically had to unhinge his jaw to stuff it all down as quickly as he was. Steve and I grabbed a soda before we pulled Kurt from the room.

The receptionist brought us to a corner office. She opened huge double oak doors. They presented an office lined by windows overlooking the New York City skyline from a hundred miles up. Everything was visible up in the clouds. The Empire State building towered. The World Trade Center were twin inspirations to the American Dream. The Statue of liberty stood grim and stolid just before turning around and giving us a cartoonish wink and a wave of her flaming torch and a welcome, welcome, and prosperity! Everything bled prosperity.

The secretary turned from us and left, closing the double doors behind her. A huge leather swivel chair faced out toward the windows, and a woman was standing beside it. A hearty guffaw cackled as the chair turned toward us. It was a forty-five year old man with thinning grey hair, smoking a smoldering cigar. The scene reminded me of the autonomous, robotic performance of John in his convalescent bed. I took all this in, but with the strange feeling of laying down half-asleep and still.

"Har, har, har, yes, yes, yes," he was addressing the svelte woman next to him. I recognized her. It was Whitney Houston. Her close-cropped curly hair and makeup made the three of us melt into the floor. She was beautiful. Positively radiant. She laughed as he continued the middle of his tirade, "and you tell your producer, no more of those expenses that have been a bit on the treif side! ha HA!"

They both started laughing.

Houston started saying something, but her throat and lips were only movin. No sound came out. She smiled, and Hirons was acknowledged what she was saying.

"Well, I will see you in three weeks. We'll start recording on that and work on the logistics of the tour." The cigar bobbed in his catfishy mouth, dropping ashes that dissipated before they hit his suit. The ashes obliterated into thin air.

Houston mouthed something.

"These guys are the new grunge act I am picking up, if everything goes as planned. 'The Dawn Ego,' and this is,... Todd?"

I raised my hand. Houston looked at me, raising an eyebrow.

"And this is Kurt and Steve," I said, pointing. "Johnny couldn't make it."

Houston mouthed something to me. I couldn't comprehend a hint of what it was.

"Yup," I mustered. She was smiling, and visibly laughed along with Hirons, even though Hirons laugh was the only one that registered aloud.

Houston mouthed again, wiggling the tips of her fingers at me in a 'goodbye' before leaving. The door closed.

"The Dawn Ego," Hirons began. His cigar was gone and he nodded his head. We all nodded our heads. He was nodding his head. We were nodding our heads. The distant Statue of Liberty nodded her head.

"The future of The Dawn Ego. The future in which you take the world by storm with your electric rock and roll, and an image that screams anarchy and revolution. Revolution for the world, and for music itself."

"You've put some thought into this," I said.

"You are going to be a brand as much as a band. Kids will want to be you, and everyone will want to listen to you."

"Sure!"

"Excellent. I really want to outline what this is going to

look like, but I also want to make sure that you are taken care of and that you are happy with our agreement. Are you going to be able to sign for Johnny, even though he isn't here?"

"We're actually going to skip Johnny."

Hirons paused, nodding.

"That doesn't entirely look good for you guys right out of the gate."

"Don't worry, it is a lot less interesting than you think - he got into a car accident and it shook him up. He said he wanted to focus on college."

"Oh. Well, best of luck to him. You're going to need a new drummer. We can help with that."

"That would be great."

"I'll make some copies of your tape, send it out to some pros, and see what we get back. At the least, we can get a studio drummer for you for your first album...which brings me to the meat of our conversation.

"The way this works is that we make up a contract with a set number of albums and tour commitments, and come to an agreement about how that is going to look and what you are going to be paid for your work. I already have something written up here."

He took several copies of a packet from a folder on his desk containing several sheets of carbon copy paper wrapped around and stapled at the top. It had a folio-pad type roll over cardstock and a blue 'Arista' on it. It felt clean and fresh, and as exciting as the first day of elementary school.

"Here's the gist of it: We want you for at least two albums and two tours. We will be given full rights to your music, but only in terms of licensing for the next twenty years. The music remains your property, the recordings ours. We can renew after that time. We'll be paying the four of you five hundred thousand dollars over the next two years, five percent royalty on the records in addition to the base cost, and we'll also be covering tour, staff, instrument, wear and tear, and other expenses when the time comes. There are some other small things - such as when I say tour, I mean your first official Arista tour, but we may be requiring you to find you and your equipment to several performances around home before we start putting you on with another band. Of course in that case we cover gas but you guys take care of lodging as long as it is within seventy-five miles.

"You'll record your first album in Nashville in three months. We already have the space booked, and we're working on sponsorship deals for instruments that you will take on tour and keep after you get them. You can record the EP songs and finally have them done professionally, or you can write new stuff. It does need to have a little bit of preapproval by the engineer and producer, so bring some extra material just in case."

Hirons looked at us with expectation, seemingly waiting for a reaction right away. I did everything I could to keep myself in check.

"That's pretty much what this document says," he tapped a fat finger on the contract. "We have a lawyer here for you to talk to if you want before you sign anything - granted, he works with us, but we aren't here to try to screw you. He'll answer any questions that you may have and I promise that he'll do it in the most honest, ethical manner.

"I had a few questions that I wasn't sure about before we go on." Hirons said, looking at a paper on the desk in front of him. "How old are you?"

"We're eighteen."

"Oh, good. Are any of you still in school?"

"Only for a few more weeks - we're pretty much done. They officially let us out of there by the end of May. It shouldn't make a difference to any of this."

"Well, just in case I'll have my secretary give you a copy of your contract and the packet to give to your school about the S.O.P. on that before you go...Questions?"

We looked at each other. Small smiles seemed to creep in the corners of Kurt and Steve's mouths. I felt like we were losing control in the moment we started to lose control of ourselves a little.

"Can we have a second to talk?"

"Absolutely. Can I get you guys anything while I step out?"

"We're good."

He left the room. He stood outside the floor to ceiling windows to the office as we celebrated. We threw papers. We knocked over the knickknacks on his desk. We danced on the chairs. We jumped on the coffee table. We jumped and hugged.

I felt like I was watching Hirons outside the room,

watching us, his back to the second me. I felt like I was rolling over and over, watching him watch us, and us jumping and hugging in a cloud of soft euphoria. It was fat and strange. It passed strange, like an out of body experience.

"This is the best possible scenario," I said to the men. "This is better!"

"I know!"

"Yes!"

"Let's do it!"

"Should we talk to the lawyer?"

"Let's just do it and figure that out later."

"I agree!"

"We'll find a drummer!"

"Let's rock!"

We hit the lottery - we literally did nothing to face this kind of success as immediately as we had, and it was almost as if we were careening toward the futures that we all felt like we deserved. We were unique and enthusiastic, our engines primed for the future.

We screamed and bounced off of one another over and over and over again. It was the success and the moment and everything.

Then, we cleaned up and opened the doors to let Hirons back in. As he walked back in, we were calm and collected.

"We're ready. Let's do it."

We signed the contract.

On the way out we loaded up all the snacks we could

carry, and another cab brought us back to the airport where we flew back home.

Hirons told us that we would be receiving our marching orders in the coming few days and performing our first shows in the coming week. He would set us up with gigs, and all we had to worry about was passing the last couple of weeks at school, getting another drummer, and showing up to the venues early and ready to play.

We made record time back to Twin Falls.

We practiced the second we arrived home. We played through our EP songs, and then set the other four or five songs that I felt were ready to perform to music and vocals. Steve was pretty sure he knew another drummer from school, and he could get him on board with joining the band to add percussion to the new songs.

"I'll bring him a tape. He'll be fine," Steve said. "I can bring him by after school tomorrow to learn the stuff so we can have a real practice on Saturday."

"Perfect," I replied.

"What about the coffee shop?" Kurt asked. "Did anyone talk to him about Saturday?" We hadn't, but it wouldn't be too difficult to tell the guy that John quit and that we needed to find another drummer. Did we even need to perform there anymore? If he was upset, it wouldn't be difficult to throw together a quick acoustic set. All exposure was good exposure.

"That should be okay - it isn't like he has a choice. Getting everyone together for a real rehearsal on Saturday is more important. That okay, Kurt?"

He nodded.

We finished up and everyone left. It was a long day of travel. Excitement. Energy. We had to take it out on our instruments before disbanding.

We needed bed.

We had school tomorrow.

Chapter 14

"So, this is the one with the three-four bridge and then the chorus again, and we end with me fading out on drums. But if we are playing live and we do it last, I'll just keep going with the bridge as a vamp and every one can solo out..."

Kermit Polpecheck sat behind his drum kit, cool and collected. He was surprisingly malleable. He was lanky skin-and-bones. He wore glasses and a ratty flannel. The method and the execution was perfect for us, even if his image was a little dorky.

His rehearsal was a fluid discovery of the songs, and as he played he riffed on John's original beat but laid some extra half beats and rim pops onto each piece. He made the songs his own. He made them better. The paint was barely dry on our freshly minted illustration of the Ouroboros with accurate presidential avatars eating themselves. It shone from the front of his bass drum head, and his beat did justice to the image.

"The kid's got it. All of it," Kurt observed.

"Yeah. Great job, Kermit. Good find, Steve," I said. "Kermit, did you hear about the contract and everything?"

"No, Steve just asked if I wanted to be in a band and that it would require a lot of time and effort. I've wanted to be in a band for a while, so whatever."

"Well, we actually have a record deal and we are recording and touring soon if everything goes according to schedule."

"I didn't want that to be the reason you joined, but... you just won the lottery, man," Steve interjected.

"You good with that?"

"Like a job?"

"Exactly like a job. This is your full time job right now."

"Good."

The day before I finished up my final responsibilities in everything except for school - and I stayed home from school in order to catch up. I resigned from Kinkos, bought and registered a car, bought some luggage for my clothes and a tour crate for my amplifier, and spoke on the phone with Hirons about our upcoming dates for shows. We had a show on Tuesday, Wednesday, Thursday, Friday, and Saturday night of the following week, so it was important to make sure Kermit was up to snuff.

Saturday came, and with it came our enthusiastic new drummer. We were well on our way to making it. The kid was fresh. He knew what he was doing after only two days, and his enthusiasm and effort made it clear he was the perfect fit. He was easy to lead, a team player, and willing to give everything up for the project.

"What do you guys think about changing our names for the sake of the band?" Steve was thinking brand, and it was practical. "You did that with John to Johnny X and I thought that was actually pretty awesome. No one is going to remember Polpechek or whatever your name is, Kermit."

"I'm with you on that," he replied with a laugh.

"Okay, so... Kermit Henson? Is that too much?"

"I like it."

"Okay. I like Kurt, but we are a little too close to another Kurt. Maybe that is brand recognition and will be good for our customer base?"

"I mean, that is my name," he responded.

"Well, yeah, but humor me for a second. Kurt Lobel. Kurt Lobel. What about Kurt Kobel? Double K thing. Or Kurt Logan?"

"Kurt Logan is cool."

"Kermit Henson, Kurt Logan, Steve Harvester · do you mind if I keep my own? Harvester is cool. And... Todd Keefe. What about Todd Irish?"

"Fine."

"Good. First names will be what sticks anyway, but..."

"How are we looking for Tuesday?" I didn't think we would have any problems, but I asked.

"Fine," Kurt replied.

"Yeah," Steve added.

"Okay. Let's call it a night. Kermit, do you want to come back the next couple nights and practice with just me to make sure you are good?"

"I'd be more comfortable with that."

"Steve, where did this guy come from?"

"Marching band."

"Perfect."

We disbanded for the evening. Everyone left.

When I finally climbed the basement stairs, Jenny was standing in the middle of the kitchen leaning on a counter. She wore a teddy and ate a piece of celery stalk. The greens at the end bounced. Her breasts hung in the red lace corset, the half-moons of her nipples popping over the hem of the demi-cup. She was radiant.

"What's up, Doc?" She bit the celery with a pop.

I walked over and grabbed her waist. I felt the ribbing on the garment tight against her body, her warmth tucked close. This was so unlike her, and that's what made it even hotter. She was a simulation of herself, doing something that grabbed my attention in the teeth and shook the life out of it. It was impossible to focus on anything but her.

"It's been days," I said. "I miss you - I need you."

"What have you been doing?"

"Securing our future, my dear." I began kissing her neck, her collarbone, and my hands molested her body. "It is done. We got a record deal, and we're rich, and we'll be touring the universe. Together."

"That sounds remarkable."

"So, you and I will be on a tour van and playing rock music and visiting all of the states and recording in Nashville. Is that okay?"

"Perfect."

She sat up on the counter and separated her legs and accepted my body against her. This counter, the same counter my family used to prepare meals was now the theater of our love making. It didn't matter.

We kissed, long and passionately. I ran my fingers over the ridges of the lace. Her body was incredibly tucked into the machine of the lingerie and I was enraptured with drinking up every inch with my fingers and my mouth. Red, red, kissing and smooth, and the glory of the moment was saturated with red.

"Where's your father been?" Mother's voice asked.

I opened my eyes, and Jenny looked at me. In her rapture, her eyes squinting with pleasure. Looked back and seemed to shake her head like, 'what?' I looked around the kitchen, and there was no one. I continued kissing her, and I answered her when I was able to retrieve my tongue.

"I don't... I haven't seen him..." Where has my father been? Why am I thinking about this now? "Business, as usual?" I kissed and kissed, and moved my lips over her neck and down to the top of her breasts. My lips trailed over the fleshy mountains, and back and forth with kisses that communicated. I communicated that this body covered in red lace was too divine for this earth. She was incredible.

"Your father is dead to us, now," Mother's voice spoke again.

"What-" I almost had a hard time stopping kissing. Jenny brushed the top of my head as my mouth travelled and sucked and I kissed her, "-did you say?"

"Your father is gone, now. He's gone forever."

"What?" I stopped kissing her and looked into her eyes, confused.

"What?" She was back to her normal voice. Was this my brain, or was it my ears from all the practice we've been doing? "Todd," and she pulled my face back into her chest.

The cups easily fell down. It appeared they were meant to. She looked amazing. She offered her symmetrical nipples to me to do my bidding. Her hair was blown out and lively, and her eyes closed and rolled back in her head. I kissed lower, and lower, and ran my face down between her legs. My mouth went to work, and I drowned in her musk.

"I need you," she breathed.

I pulled my pants all the way down and moved back up to her face. I kissed her as I tried to enter her, and it was no use. She was a wall. Dry. I thought I had spent enough time, but apparently-

"You need to be wet, too," she whispered. Without her moving from position, I bent over entirely and spit on myself. I was very close to my dick, and my spit wasn't going to help. I bent over and took the tip of my penis into my mouth. I moved down the shaft. It was big, and I had to maneuver my mouth a bit to choke it down. I was trying to spit, gravity dripping drool up my nose and across my face. I felt like if I could just unhinge my jaw it would work, and I choked my cock down some more and held it in the back of my throat until I could hardly breathe.

It was cathartic, and I never knew I could do this. I felt the muscles in my neck and my back start to ache. I released my dick, and it came slopping out of my mouth with a gooey mass of saliva gobbing off in sheets.

I unfolded myself and popped my head back up. With my eyes closed, I kissed Jenny and entered her hard and deep. She let out a surprised gasp of attention, and her pussy quickly accepted me in a slurpy mess. She moaned.

It was slow and hard, and I felt her body, and we kissed as my tempo increased to a fiery gallop. Her body was my mechanistic trap of human creation.

"Oh, Todd, honey." My mother called me, as for a favor. "Oh, dear. Heavens to Betsy." She was my mother speaking to me.

I opened my eyes and looked through the kitchen, around Jenny, and nothing. It was only Jenny. I was ramming her with my cock in an empty house. I returned my gaze to her. My eyes moved from her pussy lips hugging my penis as it pistoned in and out, up her body, and directly into her eyes. She was so hot. She breathed, her face was serious, and her mouth. The sounds, though. It all sounded as if...

As if on the center island in the kitchen, I was hammering my mother. Hammering and hammering and hammering my cock into my mother.

"What is it?" Jenny asked, or was it mother?

What?

The island began to move a little, and the hard stone of the countertop scooped down into a kind of bowl in the rock. A fuck-bowl that Jenny-Mom's ass perfectly contoured into. My eyes were popping out of my head like cylindrical daggers.

"What baby?" Jenny again, but my hip engines became uncontrollable. I was becoming the automaton, in, out, in, out, in, out, and it seemed like I couldn't control it. I was an engine. It was an engine that still wound down after the ignition was shut off.

She began shouting ecstasy, and I wildly hammered her. I didn't have a condom on. We normally wore one for birth control - and yet I couldn't stop the incessant automatic drilling.

I came, hot and decisive into her like a rush. In its power, I felt it rise in her throat as we kissed.

I felt sick. But as the image restored to normal, I was restored. Granite countertop. Jenny. Notmom. Hair amussed into a flopnest. Lingerie besoiled with sweat.

The scene dimmed. My eyes and my mind were heavy.

We showered, I think.

We went to bed, I think.

I awoke into the next week, and a rush of obligation.

The week was a trying one. Balancing school and a mini

tour wasn't that big of a deal, except for the fact that we had to get on the road. It took a few hours to get there and back with the driving, the unpacking, the performance, the load out, and then getting everything out once we were back home. We needed sleep and food. All of this was possible since everything was relatively close, but it essentially didn't leave much time for anything else.

Jenny came to Tuesday's show, but was wrecked for school on Wednesday. The band was hurting. We swam through school with black Xs on our unshowered hands and black bags under our eyes. Our bodies read like a book of adventure and sacrifice.

We made it work, and the experience was formative. It was likely what small travelling bands with day jobs had to face. We squeezed in school work when we weren't moving things or driving anywhere, and we would trade responsibilities if we needed to do our work or snooze.

The venues were similar. Dark hole in the wall with one room and some piss-dank bathrooms. When we arrived, we had to stack our equipment up in a dark corner. Then we'd watch the opening bands perform, and in between each set there was a scramble to move and assemble our gear. If we were the headliners, there was no hurry to disassemble at the end of the night.

We headlined the Tuesday and Wednesday shows, and we played just before the headliners on Thursday and Friday. It was hectic and stressful, smoky and boozy. But the audience. The genuine, screaming, appreciative, enthusiastic, and electric audience!

Hirons called on Friday afternoon just before we left for the night's show.

"Hi, Hirons, it's Todd."

"Byron?"

"Hirons."

"Byron."

"What?"

"Yes. Listen, I am hearing great things about you boys, great things. What do you think about the venues and the crowds?"

"Small, but intense. They have been great. Different than what we're used to."

"Good. I know, but it is chumpystuff." Chumpystuff? "How much school do you have left? It's time for bigger shows and the album."

"Two weeks - less? Last day is May twenty-seventh, I think. School has been the hardest part, but we'll figure it out. Only two more weeks."

"Okay. How about we get the ball rolling right after that? May twenty eight you take a plane down to Nashville for the record. Rest a couple days. If you take a week to record it, we are only talking about another two weeks turnaround for artwork and packaging - prelim, that is - for you to sell at some real shows."

"That sounds fine - I don't really need to go to graduation, but the guys might want to. I can double check. This sounds like a reasonable request, though... Is it normal for a band to record an album in a week?"

"No, but I think you guys can do it."

"Okay."

"Spackle!" Spackle? "And I have here a date for your first few post-recording shows in a couple weeks. For the most part you're going to be filling in on other tours where the original opening acts dropped out. I tried to get you on some grunge bills, but a few of them are whatever we can fill. There are two reasons for that - one, is that we're simply trying to get you exposure, and two is that record companies usually try to get their own bands on the same bill to save money, save on promoter costs, vans, equipment, whatever."

"Okay."

"So here they are. We have you opening for a band called 'Radiohead' on December sixth in Boston, another a few days later with a band 'Toadies,' the next day, a band called 'Bush,' which is funny because you're actually covering for Toadies who couldn't be there that night-"

"-wait."

"What?"

"I am confused."

"Okay, about what?"

"You said we would be going to record the album in a couple weeks, but then that we are opening for these bands in a couple weeks."

"Precisely."

"Okay."

"What?"

"Well, we have dates we are talking about here, right? I'm confused."

"What are you confused about?"

And then I saw Hirons. I saw him in his office.

He was tapping a pencil on a pad. His secretary was sucking his dick under his desk. He looked down at his lap and shook his head, pointing to his phone. 'Can you believe these guys?' he communicated. The secretary shrugged with the cock in her mouth for a moment, and continued bobbing. The tight curls of her red hair bounced like a pompom.

Was it me?

"Okay, so you said you are flying us down in a couple weeks," I said, "and we're both talking about May twenty-eighth."

"Yes."

"Ninety-four? And the first show we are doing with this 'Radio Head' or whatever is December sixth, this year?" I enunciated my words. "Which you said is also two weeks away?"

"Don't worry about the logistics, Todd. We'll have it all taken care of. Just don't late." What? His grammar was even a mess.

"I'm afraid we'll too early."

"Talk sense, Todd. If I were you, I would be afraid of being too curly," and over the phone I heard him waggle his eyebrows at the secretary who pushed his swivel chair backward until it 'tinked' the plate glass window. Without taking his dong out of her mouth, she flipped herself backward and around. Her pelvis landed at his head, and her feet landed on the glass. Her skirt lifted with the gymnastic feat. Her pink, shaved pussy landed in his face.

"Let's touch base in a couple weeks and see where we are at," he continued. He cleared his throat. "YUMYUMYUMYUMYUM!" His voice became cartoonish as he began devouring her, the words popping in comical fonts over his head. Todd heard squishing of muscle and flesh over the receiver.

"Okay," He replied. He didn't entirely know what he had agreed to, nor what the appropriate phone etiquette was in this particular circumstance.

"Don't miss your gigs over the next couple weeks." Hirons managed to eke out. He breathed in through his nose as he bit. Bone and cartilage crunched, blood sopping from his mouth and soaking his suit. "Good. Buy. Todd."

"Goodbye, Mr. Hirons."

"Byron Wyman!"

The line went dead, and on the other end Hirons and the secretary ate, and ate, and ate.

Until, pop!

They were no more!

Chapter 15

The recording studio in Nashville was wood. Cathedral ceilings breathed. Thousands of mechanistic and oppressive slats of wood were individually installed on the walls and the ceiling and the floor by hand. The room was a grinder with wooden bars that would collapse like a mandolin egg slicer at any moment.

Soon the slats would slice.

We stood with our instruments.

Microphones stood around the room, and cables, and everything was far away from everything else.

"Okay, I think we're ready," I began.

We were frozen still. Silence. The vapid void of nothing sucked by the room's acoustics. There was nothing - no movement, and all as statuary. All sound dissipated into blackness between the wooden slats.

"The Dawn Ego, track one, take one," I said, because that's what I thought I was supposed to say... Or the engineer was supposed to say it.

"...and then," the engineer said.

I didn't understand.

"And then, what?"

Click, "...and then,"

There was no movement from behind the glass. They were wax figures with unmoving mouths. It was difficult to see behind the glass, but they were like Gerry Anderson puppets in a ship staring from the space window. They were twice removed from us by thick double panes of glass, tinted just so. They were in another plastic universe.

"And then, what?" I repeated.

"And then," click, "and then," click, "and then," click, "and then," click "and then," click "and then," click, like a metronome, tick, tick, tick, and then, and then, and then.

I turned to Kurt who was standing stock still stunned, his mouth only open a tiny crack, and I noticed some of the sound came from his mouth hole, "and then, and then, and then," in complete synchronization. The sound was nothing like a voice, though. There was no movement of air, like a treble-cackle from a fast food drive through speaker, "and then, and then, and then, and then,"

I walked to Steve, my knees wobbly and unsure, and everything felt dizzyingly strange and new. Steve's plasticene marionette shell was like everyone else's.

He continued, "and then, and then, and then, and then..."

I had a hard time breathing, like I was carrying around a metal railroad spike in the middle of my chest and I had to make room for all my organs.

"and then, and then, and then, and then,"

Tick, tock, tumbling about the time, turning down three hours to one, and two weeks to take turns talking.

"and then, and then, and then, and then,"

AND THEN, AND THEN, I KNOW, I KNOW!

"and then, and then, and then, and then,"

Always knocking, never stopping,

"and then, and then, and then,"

And the ceiling's gears began its grinding descent, as in the distance I heard our music. Softly, softly.

"and then, and then, and then, and then,"

and the wood creeeeeaked like a pine being squeaked against its own moist innards to wrench down a branch, or even better, the chalky clack and squeak of birches softly swaying in the winter and landing together to rub, rub, rub it out,

"and then, and then, and then, and then,"

and the wood kept coming closer, as if the interlocking mechanics of it was built for this one purpose. It was a recording studio that could fold into nothingness, compact and transportable and ready to take in a briefcase in a moment's notice. The wooden clockwork was engineered to do this one task: to enfold into itself.

"and then, and then, and then, and then,"

When the slats reached my bandmates, it cut into them like egg with nary a reaction from anyone in fleshy shiny slices. They were aspic. So it did the same with our amplifiers in licorice sheen, and the momentum continued the cut toward me.

"and then, and then, and then, and then"

and our music got louder, it screamed, and I lay on my back. Limbo lower, if only I could breathe, and it stifled me as it pressed into my ribcage and began to compress it.

"and then, and then,"

There was a little snap.

Painless, really.

It sliced, and I felt my yolk spill as I closed my eyes.

I was holding my breath.

Longer.

Precise and long.

Compressed and salient, salty dough.

Pressed firmly through, squeezed through, pushed and squeezed through the other side.

Our music.

A fushhhhhhhhh like snow on a television.

Da-de-dah dah. Baddah,

one-

    two-

        three-

      one-

        two-

          three.

Breathe in, goddamnit!

And I did, and the snow sound pushed through the other side of the floor into the cheer of thousands? Hundreds? Disoriented, and feeling here, jolted awake and hot, hot, hot.

Black floor, spilled beer, dark room. I did everything to get up, and spun around. The stickiness of gaffer's tape up my arm; rotten, old, and putty that won't come off for days. On my hands and knees, and something coming off my arm.

Mic cord. The mic cord was wrapped around my arm, and I wrenched it free.

A needle. A needle hung and swung, and drool dripped down from my mouth.

Hands and knees, dizzy and malformed.

I moved from my hands and knees a little to the left to gain my footing, and my guitar swung from behind me and hit the stage, Bawwwwwwwww, until I grabbed it with my needlearm and muffled the strings.

Standing, standing.

I took hold of the mic stand, and the cheers grew.

The room was different. Poles, poles, I was on a stage and there were silver poles, and heads. Black snakes stretched to the black ceiling from the poles. Heads and poles, and lights! Oh glory, the lights.

The room was electric. Hundreds of bodies bounced, and hair clung and hung from sweaty foreheads, holding on to one another and reforming the sea-crowd of heads with the humming heat and happy happy holiday of our song.

It was December sixth.

And so our song played and played and played, the band riffed true against the maelstrom of crowd and rock and everything that was here that was so true.

It was, in fact, December, and Hirons Byron Wyman had taken care of everything for us before he ate his secretary and she ate him. That was the best situation a guy could hope for. Sexual obliteration.

To my left, Steve was in a trance, hopping through his riffs with scientific accuracy. His eyes rolled into his skull.

And then, Kurt was wailing on through his rhythms, apparently waiting for his solo.

And then, Kermit was popping through his kit in perfect mastery of syncopation, robotic in scope but ragging the three-four time just enough for it to sound human.

And there were horns to my right where a trombone and a trumpet were screaming. And a woman jumped to the stage and had a bottle of whiskey. Jumping in time, grabbed the trumpet's mute and filled it to the top with bourbon. She tore her shirt from her body. Black bra and a big black ouroboros tattoo across her chest, she winked at me and chugged the bourbon from the cup of the mute. With an arm in the air, still jumping and still jumping, her breasts jiggled in waves and her eyes were mesmerizing and hypnotic.

Our eyes connected for a moment. My heart pounded. I could have sworn we smiled and cried. She turned, dropped the empty mute, and jumped into the crowd.

and then, I ripped the needle out of my arm because it felt like an orgasm with her and with everyone, everywhere. I picked up the neck of my guitar, swimming in sex.

and then, I turned the knob on the guitar to ten.

and then, I made my G with my left hand.

and then, I laid down into the strings with heroic power, stretching my arm straight down into the chordal cream and pulling up the harmonious gods from the depths of hell to join us on stage.

and then, the waves of audience were waves like pixels and stars moving like haunts with the melodies. Kurt began jumping, laying into his guitar as he melodramatically joined in with melodious machinations.

and then, the beat locked in as Kermit slam, slam, slammed into his drum, drums, drums. The beat, beat, beating with passion, shun, shun.

and then, I pulled the needle out of my arm.

and then, Steve powered in, ba-doom, doom-ba-doom, doom-ba-doom-ba-doom, becoming the sex, the baseless intercourse undercurrent and through the bodies of the people. They were ecstatic and true, and all the watts the bass powered into them with waves and vibrations that were more true to them than their own hearts. More true than their hearts, can you believe it!? Mercy.

and then, I pulled the needle out of my arm.

and then, I powered and strummed, and there was a little blinking red light in the light and sound booth. I stared at it while I played, and mascara and black eyeliner ran down my face, and I saw it at the same time, and I was a big face and all of this was happening too fast, way too fast, and the light and the sound pumped like a heart.

and then the crowd was a big heart, and I beat with it.

and then, I pulled the needle out of my arm.

and then, the song crescendoed in strength, power, and tempo.

and then, I turned in front of the crowd.

and then, I pulled the needle out of my arm.

and then, I jumped backward.

and then, I fell.

Chapter 16

Out of the darkness.

I opened my eyes.

Everything seemed clear.

White.

Verywhite.

Bright verywhite.

Pockmarked ceiling tiles.

Here are ceiling tiles.

I can count twenty four ceiling tiles.

Swirling around the ceiling tiles were metal tracks.

My mouth was full. My mouth was so very full.

Psst, a machine whispered next to me. The machine had a bag, regulating fluid.

The line trailed down, clear and magnified fluid, around

the bedframe, down into my arm.

I used my arm to pull what was in my mouth out. I removed a long, plastic corrugated tube that I felt moving straight down to the center of my chest. I yanked it free followed with a drizzle of drool, and heavy warm air filled my lungs like sacks of rice.

On my arm, there wasn't a needle missing. There was a needle there. There was a needle attached to the bag.

I looked down my arm and I saw the needle, and beyond it I saw my hand. I lifted my arm a little, moving my fingers, and-

beepbeepbeepbeepbeepbeepbeep

-an alarm went off and there was something wrong with the arm I was looking at. It was disproportionate and strange.

"I swear, Keefe," a large black woman in tye dye scrubs entered in the middle of focusing on putting on her rubber gloves, "if you've pulled that butterfly catheter out one more time, I am gonna duct-tape that got-da-" She paused, mid-stride, staring at me. My hand was still in the air.

"Hello," I whispered. It hurt.

"Hello," she said. Her eyes grew wide. Her finger touched a blue button and the alarm stopped. She walked directly over to me and started to take my blood pressure. There was a little cart she brought over with a box on it - some kind of huge thermometer with disposable tips and curly telephone wires everywhere.

Some hospital.

She looked at her watch, and intently tapped a clipboard

on the thermometer cart like she was rudely waiting for me to finish my temperature.

Was it rude? She looked like she was concentrating on the tapping.

"Okay, honey, everything looks good, but I am going to ask you to not move. I need to call the doctor. I'll be back in a minute, and then we can talk."

She left the room, and the machine next to me gave a 'psst,' and then a 'rowr' of a motor. I heard another 'psst' to my left. I turned my head, and there was a man sleeping very still with the same setup. Straight across from me, another three beds on the opposite side of the room. All sleeping patients. On my right, another bed with a woman.

The rest of the room was sparse. Behind each bed there were wall hookups and a little canister thing with tubing - maybe a vacuum. In one corner of the room near the door was a counter with a sink, a sharps container, and some medical supplies. On the other end of the big room, there was a big metal cabinet.

Where was the bathroom?

I laid my head back down. I traced my eyes across the ceiling, imagining little trains running along the interconnected tracks swirling about. There were connections. Everyone was busy. The Orient Express wound through a wintry mountain range with cups of tea barely moving in the dining car.

The woman walked back in. She pulled a wheely stool next to my bed.

"Okay, so I'm here to talk. The doctor can tell you more when he arrives. Do you want to talk with me, or wait?"

"No... I sort of know why I'm here." She pulled the cart with the thermometer and the clipboard. She started touching it, again.

"What do you remember?"

"Listen, I don't have a drug problem. I've never done them, but somehow with the show... It doesn't make sense. Worst I've ever done was sip some of my dad's beer on a football night or something."

My voice sounded like shit. It was raspy and deathly from the bottom of a crypt. I really must have been screaming, or hungover. Does heroin make you hung over?

"What do you remember happening?"

"I was on stage. We were playing and I had a needle in my arm. That is all I remember. I did some drugs. I fell off the stage..." My eyes searched my sheets in front of me, looking for the answer.

"Oh. So there were drugs involved?"

"I guess. I don't know where they came from, so if that is the next question ·"

"No, it isn't honey." She looked at the clipboard in front of her and ran her hand across it intently. It seemed to glow? "Do you remember a van ride?"

"I'm in a band."

"John Xiong was driving a van?" She was reading off the clipboard. "You were riding in back?"

"Yeah. Van was wrecked, John quit. We moved on."

A man walked in with determination.

"Hello, Todd, I am Doctor Krishnamurthy. I am a doctor on duty here at Saint Lucius Hospital. I hear you're awake and doing well."

He produced a flashlight and checked my pupils.

"Yes, I feel good. Rested."

"Excellent. Can you tell me why you're here?"

"Drugs...and I fell off a stage."

He took the flashlight down and looked me in the eyes, and then at the nurse.

"That's what he told me," she said.

"Do you mind?" He motioned to the stool and the woman stood. Dr. Krishnamurthy sat beside the bed. "Do you do drugs, Mr. Keefe?"

"Never before then."

"What kind of drugs were they, Mr. Keefe?"

"Heroin?"

"I see." He took out a gadget, attached a black cap to it and began looking in my nose and ears. "Mr. Keefe, there are no traces of drugs in your system. I guarantee it."

"That's a relief."

"Yes, as a matter of fact, aside from a few minor indicators, you are in very good health and you are incredibly lucky."

"Oh yeah?"

He looked at me gravely, and we kept eye contact. He took

the clipboard from the nurse.

"He seems lucid and aware of his surroundings," he said to the nurse. She tapped. "This is Betty, she is the nurse on duty for your room, but she will be bringing you to another room shortly. Tell me, what is it you last remember?"

"I was just telling Betty - taking my drugs and falling off a stage."

"That did not happen, Todd. You were in an accident, and you have been here under our care since the accident. Do you know where you are?"

"You just said -" He said we were at Saint Lucius. I was in Boston. "Saint Lucius? Twin Falls, Saint Lucius?"

"You were in an accident..." he looked at the glowing clipboard. "April twenty-second, 1994."

"Okay. Sure. That was our first show, when that guy crashed into the van and almost killed us all."

"You remember, then?" He flipped it back to Betty, and once again she tapped her fingers on it.

"Yeah, like ages ago."

"Ages ago?"

"Well, touring for the last three weeks," my voice was horse, "although some of it makes no sense in there because we had a show in June, but then it was December already and we played with Radio Head."

"Radiohead."

"That is what I said. And we were in Boston. What, did I get air flighted here or something? Did Hirons pay for it to get me closer to my family?"

A smile edged the corner of Betty's face, the red lipstick shone in the dim light of the room.

"I'm afraid to tell you some things that may come as a shock to you. We're here for whatever support you need."

"Okay," I said slowly.

"What year is it?"

"Ninety-four."

"Mr. Keefe, the year is twenty-nineteen. It has been twenty-five years since your accident."

My mind was blank. In any other circumstance, it seems that I would be angry, or upset. I was confused, but mostly, I was just... Blank.

"You were the sole survivor of the accident. A drunk driver hit your vehicle. John Xiong was killed instantly and Steven Harvester was ejected and died later. Your van was pushed up and over the barricade over Snake River, and the van fell into the gorge. The van then took on water, with you and Kurt unconscious in the back. Kurt Lobel drowned in the van. The van sank in such a way that you were found above water on boxes in the back of the van.

"You are a very lucky man, Todd. I know that this is going to be a difficult process for you-"

"No."

"No, what?"

"No..." I was trying to be patient. "I get it."

"Okay. We are going to make sure you have a therapist

and neurologist available as a part of your treatment. There is something else we need to talk about right away, however."

I sat stony and still. He took an instrument out of his lab coat along with a little rubber hammer. The instrument looked like a tiny pizza cutter with spikes instead of a blade. He held them in his hands between his knees as he addressed me.

"This is a lot of information to process, and it will take time. I'm afraid there's no better way to say this, Todd. In the accident you were gravely injured, and you have come a long way in twenty-five years. You have battled some things that I am sure you didn't even know you were battling. It says in your chart you had a near fatal bedsore that I am sure you still have scarring from... In the accident you had three broken ribs. A fracture of your right orbital bone behind your eye. A broken tibula. Four bones broken in your foot. Hemorrhaging everywhere, namely in your face. You were a mess.

"You also fractured a few other bones that were a little more important than these. Of course, all of your bones are important, but some are those we can not fix. You fractured cervical vertebrae four, five, and six. You fractured thoracic vertebrae one and two. You shattered almost all of your lumbar vertebrae.

"The medical team that assisted you did a fantastic job with you. You were brought in on a back board, and they immediately went to work stabilizing you, many surgeries to put some hardware back there to keep everything from falling apart. It was bad, but not impossible."

"So?"

"We're pretty certain of some things. Before I say anything, I would like to check if that's okay?"

He took his little hammer, and bonked by right knee. I braced for the uncomfortable shock and reaction.

It didn't come.

Nothing.

He did it two more times.

He switched to my left knee.

Three times.

Nothing.

"Betty, note reflex hammer elicits no response."

He put his hammer back in his pocket and took out the spiky pizza cutter.

"Your only job is to react as you feel this instrument. Tell me if and when you feel it, and I am going to ask that you stare at the ceiling or close your eyes as I complete this test.

I looked up at the ceiling and closed my eyes.

Twenty five years.

I've been on tour for twenty five years?

I've been away for twenty five years.

I have eaten myself and been reborn, chewing on my years. I've been a waif for twenty-five years.

Just yesterday, I was worried about what was next, and what was next, and so much potential. It seemed as though it was guaranteed to some degree, and then...

No, I have to get out of here. This is some sick -

I grabbed the bed railing, but then held my hand in front of me. The skin was distended, floppy, and pale. There were brown marks that hadn't been there. My bones showed through the grey flesh, and the muscles seemed weak. The fingernails had ridges running lengthwise that weren't so before. Grey hairs peeked from the sleeve of my blue johnnie robe like brush on the side of the highway, or the bottom of Snake River Canyon.

"Where are my friends?"

There was a pause.

"They died in the accident."

"Does my mom know I am awake? ˙ow!" there was a pain to the side of my right thigh near my testicles. "˙the fuck?"

I looked down at the doctor, and he looked up at me from where he sat on the stool. He turned his attention to Betty.

"Reaction anterior right thigh, approximately four inches from mid coxal?" He paused. "Todd, I am so sorry."

"No ... I know, I...understood what you were saying, but you can just tell me."

"Your mother and father. I don't want to me bringing you all of this news at once, but I also don't want to lie to you."

"I thought you were going to tell me that I can't-" and I looked at my legs.

He didn't say anything.

"While you were in the coma and recovering, we've been under the impression that you are not going to be able to walk."

"Oh."

"We are going to do everything we can, though. May I

continue?"

"Yes."

"Beginning left foot."

My eyes were back on the ceiling. Twenty five years, and this ceiling. The only thing I could look at was this ceiling, even if I had opened my eyes.

Mother. Mother and father. The fountain of my existence. I knew they were gone.

It was immediate.

There was a feeling of momentum that began to grow in me that I was falling toward some abyss of terrible news. It was a horrendous terror at the bottom of a cliff, and I stood at the precipice with an understanding that these horrors would be screaming up at me like demons. An earthly hell, horrible and unimaginable, and banking toward me with all manner of industrious news of suffering, death, and new griefs that would open their mouths and swallow me whole.

It began with these spikes, prodding me and pushing me in places I cannot even feel - and that, a new horror, the horror of nothing or the horror of the lack of feeling anything. The horror of emptiness and apathy, numbness and dissolution. Dissolution of self, as my feeling creeps up with this tool writing a numb, bloody history up my legs.

This emptiness grew. It was a nothing that spread through my brain. It was a cancer of negative space. It was a hole, or a series of holes growing rapidly and exponentially, joining like bubbles to meld together in one dual-sphere of emptiness. One began in my heart. Cold. Cold nothing. Empty as lungs, a cavity of air and void of all emotion.

The ceiling. There. That is a constant.

Oh, and how I couldn't perform anymore? Like a real rock star? Who ever heard of the rockin' wheelchair man? The wheel in the sky is now the wheels beside my thighs, propelling me to nothingness and insignificance. I felt it in my legs.

My life is over.

"Ow!"

"Anterior left thigh in line with the right, about four inches mid coxal." Betty tapped tapped tapped her clipboard thing. "Do you have any questions?"

"Can I walk?"

"No."

"Are you leaving?"

"I will be leaving soon, but I will see you again. I need to write up a lot now that you're up. Meanwhile, you're getting a room. Your nurse will get you anything you need in the meantime."

"Can I have some paper?"

He nodded to Betty and gave me his pencil. The pencil was strange and made of some kind of wax. I tried to dig my fingernail into it, but the dent healed.

"...and a mirror?"

"There will be one in your new room."

We stared at one another for a minute.

He was a stranger.

"I'll be leaving and Betty will wheel you down to the third floor. From here we are going to get you moving and keep an eye on your gastrointestinal and renal systems as we transition away from the liquid diet and get you vertical. We will also be keeping an eye on your circulation. You'll continue on blood thinners to prevent clots from forming, but wean you off those eventually as well.

"Now we focus on undoing everything that we've had to do over the past twenty five years to keep you alive. Your parents have taken great care of you, though, and that is something to be thankful for. They listened to our interpretation of your GCS data, visited all the time, and followed us along with any new data or treatment changes. They always believed you would be waking from this. They were right.

"They also made sure everything would be paid for. The only thing you need to worry about here is getting better. We will keep you here for the least possible amount of time, and then get you over to rehab. Hopefully this is speedy and painless. We'll keep a close eye on you to make sure you have a speedy recovery."

"Thank you, doctor."

"Anything else?"

"No."

"At the very least, the good news is that you're not a heroin addict."

He left with Betty, and I stared at the ceiling. The pocks in the panels swam, moved, and dissolved.

The empty, the nothing, filled and extended beyond by body. The weight was the gravity of a supernova in a galaxy far away. I was the center; the dense, heavy mass of everything. As the explosion expanded in the form of my emerged consciousness, so did matter collect at the core of my ever-expanding void of nothingness. Heavy, heavy, heavy dense matter, and it attracted more.

Watching the ceiling, I could only think that nothing would escape the density of my despair; not even light.

Chapter 17

"So, the remote is right here on this cord. This button is to call me if you need anything. This button is for the light above your bed. These work the television. The sound comes from the little speaker here."

The young, strawberry blonde nurse bent over the bed. Her breast lightly touched the top of my arm as she showed me the remote. I felt a stirring. It was good to know that everything wasn't broken.

"Where's the TV?" I asked.

"What?"

"The television?"

"On the wall."

I saw a terrible pastel photo of a vase of flowers, and a chalkboard on a pivoting hinge.

"Look." She pushed the power button, and the chalkboard came to life with a show.

"What?"

"Oh. Oh, I see. Yes. Yes, televisions are flat - they don't have the old ones anymore. Better for the environment. Look," and she showed me her clipboard. It was a little screen with my charts on it. There were no wires. She showed me how she could write on it with her finger, and switch screens like on Windows, but without a mouse. It was the same clipboards that Betty and Krishnamurthy were preoccupied with in the coma room.

"...and it just - you walk around with this?"

"Yeah, it has everything. Always updated on the network with everyone's records."

"The network?"

"Yeah, wireless. Did you have the Internet?"

"Yeah. There's a modem in there, or something?"

"A modem?"

"Hmm..."

"Listen, I have to visit the rest of my patients again. Press that button if you need anything, okay?"

"I thought that was a chalk board," I said, pointing to the television.

"Chalk board?"

"Before you go, the doctor said there would be a mirror?"

She flipped up a little box on my tray table, and sure enough there was a little glass mirror built in. Some things don't change.

"Thanks."

She left. I didn't even get her name.

I turned up the volume on the television. A newscaster was speaking.

I pulled the tray table up to my stomach and adjusted the height of the back of the bed with the controls so I was sitting up. My balance was strange. My legs were almost in the way, anchoring me down, and yet failing to be an anchor point. I felt like I was going to tip over and slump to the side. After leaning my butt over in one direction, I managed to stay vertical.

The mirror was a narrow sliver of silver, and required a little bit of tooling around to get my face into position to see it. A flash of skin, a toss of hair, and finally I was able to see a glint of myself reflected in the small rectangle.

It was horrifying. I teetered on the edge.

I first saw my eyes. Once blue, the eyes that looked back at me were grey and glassy. They looked like I had been staring at the sun, and crying, and sucking the life out of everyone's party and leaving it to distill and fade in the sunlight. The color was gone. Bags hung in heavy wrinkles around my eyes.

My cheeks were sallow, my eye sockets and jawline were skeleton-like. My skin hung into jowls on my thin face. It wasn't used to the new gravity. I looked tired - I was tired! I wasn't sick, but there was no question that there was a lack of tone and definition to my facial muscles. I had wasted away to nothing. I was nothing on the outside, and I was filling with nothing. I remained nothing but a skin soaked skeleton.

My teeth looked good. Untouched by any food for ages, they remained immaculate piano keys. They were somewhat discolored. There were wrinkles around my mouth, though. My mouth was crepe-paper skin tossed haphazardly on a frame of a face. Alas poor Todd, I knew him Horatio. I held my own skull on my neck.

I maneuvered my gaze up to the top of my head. My hair was a brambly wisp. Much of what was there had fallen out at some point. Single hairs danced in the air from my pate while a crown of sparse fur encircled the poor fading twilight above my ears.

I looked old.

The nothingness spread, and I felt old and that I had lost myself to the sentence of going too fast, too young. What was there to show for it but old age and trembling fear of whatever was left of my sentence on this earth.

What was left?

It seemed that I wanted to go back.

I wanted to go back to the incomprehensible strangeland of fame and youthful exploration of the fantasy dream state that I was living in for the past twenty five years. It seemed like only a couple weeks. It was my familiar world, filled with the dreams of my youth, and making it, and art, and music, and potential, potential, potential.

But this? This was another story altogether. I was nothing. I was broken and shattered in an empire of nothing. I would be leaving here in a wheelchair and learning how to live my life all over again. Not only that, but I had never lived my life as a...forty year old? I had never done anything to deserve this, and would I have had any idea about what I should have been doing? Or how? It was ridiculous.

I wanted to get up and run, but I couldn't. I could only stare at my old wrinkleyes, and a male pattern baldness that I had no choice but to accept.

"...coming up on the twentieth anniversary of 9/11. President Bush wants to commemorate and defend his tactics in the years leading up to the wars in the Middle East..." the announcer said on the television. "...and there are new developments in the length the troop will be staying in Iraq after the second round of increases that President Obama ordered five years ago..." A black man signed papers and flashbulbs popped.

It was hard to believe they were still talking about Bush defending Kuwait almost thirty years later. But there was much to learn - a healthy method of coping with my new surroundings and driving away this growing astral nothingness that ate away at my existence.

My health, and the events of the last twenty five years.

There was a lot of programming on the little blackboard television. Most of my favorite shows were no longer on. Music was no longer on MTV, nor was The Real World. Television seemed entirely comprised of normal people going about their business and competing with other normal people to do a variety of normal things that didn't match real world conditions - and the winner got some kind of recognition? It reminded me of a show that a British exchange student that stayed with us for two weeks one year got in a shipment on videotape – Eurovision. But everything on television was like Eurovision. But plain. Plain Eurovision all of the time. Approvision.

When we watched Eurovision, there was something trashy that stood out about the songs in English. It was around that time that I dedicated my life to making music, pledging that my band would never sound like any of the wallpaper music on the junk tape that night.

But today there was no band. There wasn't even a tape. I had been told in conversation that there weren't tapes anymore. Or even CDs. It all came in the air, wirelessly. I learned vinyl was back.

What a strange world.

I learned a lot watching television and speaking with my physical and occupational therapists. While I learned how to lift myself in and out of my wheelchair and strengthen my muscles, I also learned that we had elected a black president. A black president. It felt more of a feverdream than the coma, and I was able to deduce that the years of his presidency were remarkably stable. I also learned that I mistook the president Bush that was in the newscast - that George Bush's son was also elected to be president, and that he started a perpetual war in the Middle East that was fought through the entirety of my coma.

I also learned that I was feeling more and more depressed. In this blackness and repetition, there was no end to the suffering that began the moment I woke up. I remained incarcerated in my body. I was feeling as though I had given up before anything started.

But I think it was because it never started.

Nothing in this world is guaranteed.

Nothing in this world is wonderful and sacred, and one must understand that to take the world for what it is, they need to take advantage of everything they can while they can. One mustn't compromise for anything. The world is beautiful, disgusting, heartbreaking, wonderful, tragic, wholesome, and an absolute whore. We're going to die anyway.

Twenty five years ago, I hadn't taken advantage of anything. I only scratched the surface, and my future was snatched from me regardless of the circumstances I thought I would be in only a few months from the accident. It was a fiction.

I would have preferred the fiery drug-fueled coma death to this.

But this... I was a man in a wheelchair. My existence surrounded everything I could and couldn't do in that chair. My hair, my appearance, my wrinkles and cacking voice would be nothing more than demerits to my character. I had never been so vain in my life as the moment I was resigned that I no longer had anything to be vain about. The enthusiastic and optimistic me was never coming back. Old, feeble, and crippled was my sentence.

And so, the nothingness grew. The light faded, sucked into the inescapable maw of a black hole heart. What was next? Death.

Over the next four weeks, doctors wanted to make sure that I was able to eat solid food and use the bathroom on my own prior to allowing me to leave to the next rehabilitation step.

I learned how to do these things.

I also learned that there was a trust set up for me that was paying for my medical treatment, insurance, and the family home and its upkeep. I just had to get better. I began looking forward to each marker and milestone.

My spirit improved when I was transferred to the rehab center. It was like a nursing home attached to the hospital. Most of my neighbors were the elderly and the terminally ill.

The place was depressing, masked in a design that barely resembled an Italian villa. The halls had beautifully constructed oval archways, elegant crown molding, and large exotic fish tanks. Foliage dotted the halls, and dining rooms were silverwared and tableclothed. Scratched beneath the veneer at every turn were little signs of hospital. I rolled everywhere on industrial linoleum tile, and occasionally passed a crane for lifting and hosing off patients. Plastic bumper rails bordered every wall so gurneys wouldn't destroy the plaster.

It was beautiful. It was horrific.

My roommate was Ester. Ester had a stroke seven years ago when she was eighty nine, and perpetually remained in rehab.

Ester got up every morning, put on her makeup in the mirror, and spent the rest of the day in her wheelchair kicking herself around our floor. She wore a solid inch of red lipstick around her mouth that nearly bordered the bottom of her nose to the top of her chin. Her eyeliner that appeared to be applied with a fat-tipped magic marker. It was sixties mod-clown-horror.

No one ever came to visit Ester. Photos on her side table featured two young couples and their children. Until the morning I finally addressed her, I thought she was mute.

"You really slathered it on this morning, Ester." I don't know why I said it. I was in a frisky and optimistic mood, eating my breakfast in front of the television watching the news cycle repeat for the sixth time.

"Yes."

She looked at me, her gigantic Joker-smile wildly careening from one end of her mouth to the other. Her lipstick was applied in a moving car for twenty hours. Her eyes literally popped from dark, skeletal sockets.

I stopped mid-chew, the gelatinous eggs sitting disgustingly against my pallet, shivering along with my nervous tongue. It was one of the first solid foods I could eat before I could leave the hospital. Whatever this egg product was, it wasn't anything to look forward to after eating through my arm for so long. I swallowed.

"I'm sorry, Ester."

"Yes."

"For some reason I thought you were catatonic or something. I don't know why. I think it's because you haven't talked with anyone the whole time you've been here. Not the nurses, not family, not me. Although I know I have only been here for a week, or so.

"Anyway, I'm Todd. I was in an accident, and then I was in a coma for a very long time, and now I can't walk. I need to figure it out from here. They need to make sure I'm healthy enough to live on my own.

"If you need anything, let me know."

"Yes." Her head bobbed pleasantly. A smile. I could have said anything.

We became great friends. I learned that she was a tremendous listener that I could unload on whenever I was having a bad day. Ester could only say "yes" because of her stroke, and she needed my attention as much as I needed her affirmation.

Thom was the other connection I made in rehab. He was my physical therapist, gigantic at seven and a half feet tall. He had long, dark brown hair and the look of a Samoan who was two steps away from murder.

Thom approached physical therapy like a drill sergeant. Every moment of my therapy, four hours a day in their efforts to get me out of the hospital as soon as they could, brought shouts and tasks hammered at a speedy clip. It was stressful and liberating. I felt the progress I was making at the end of each day.

"...and I somehow need to push myself up from my chair and reach over to that bar and let myself down on the toilet? What if it rolls away?"

"YOU PINSY-ASS FECK," and when he shouted, his

south Pacific accent shone like daggers in his deep voice, "HOW A'YOU WORRY ABOUT THE WHEELCHAIR ROLLING AWAY WIT' PISS DRIBBLIN' DAWN YA LEG WAITIN' TA' LONG IN THE DRUG STORE LINE TO BUY YOUR TAMPONS?! GET DA'DICK OUT'CHA MOUTH, LIFT YA'SELF UP, AND SIT ON DA CAN."

Of course I ended up doing it. Sitting on the toilet, it became apparent that I had nothing to worry about.

"Well! I did it," I observed optimistically.

"Yes, y'did," he replied. When I wasn't working toward some goal in my therapeutic process, he turned into a gigantic, burly puppy dog. His eyes turned from bulging red marbles to cool brown orbs. His accent lessened, and his voice warmed. "Let me know if is too much. Sometime you need some motivation. I can turn it off if you need."

"Sure."

"You had good coach in high school?"

"I didn't like sports."

"Well, you have good coach now."

At the end of our sessions, he would pump a meaty hand toward me and wrap his arm around me in a burly hug. He was all business, but as much of a snugly bunny as he was a tough stone.

Thom taught me many methods of maneuvering my new lot in life. He helped me tone my muscles as much he helped to tone my mind to take on my new challenges. Never had there been anything so difficult in this life, and I hadn't even started.

This life. Starting this life...

When my mind wandered down this lane, I had the most difficulty.

I was in the rehabilitation center and hospital for six months of my forty-third year. If I lived to be seventy-five, that meant that I only had a little over thirty years left of existence. I used up half the time left I had on this earth in a hospital. I was in a coma for more of my life than I was not. Most of that time wouldn't be usable. It wouldn't be anything but wheelchair and discrimination and sexless sorrowful loneliness.

Bill was my useless therapist. He waas everyone's therapist in the rehab center, and went room to room for his sessions. He had asked if I had considered ruminating on the small moments that I had that made life worthwhile. I had very little that I could consider to be worthwhile small moments. Was one overcoming needing help with taking a shit? Or bathing while someone stood there with me? Learning that my dreams were completely dead at this point, or that the life I have lived with fame and enjoyment and fulfillment was nothing more than a coma dream? Hell, even the mundane was depressing - Michael Jackson was dead. Michael fucking Jackson.

"I never realized that you were a fan," he responded.

"I wasn't."

"Well?"

"Well, I mean, I listened to Thriller so many times as a child that the tape wore out and my mom needed to buy me another. I guess I was a fan. But you know, over the years his escapades with the law and the tabloids and his getting whiter and whiter, or whatever... I thought everyone lost patience."

"You know, Todd, they gave him an autopsy. He died because he had overdosed on drugs administered to him by his doctor. Turns out he actually had vitiligo universalis - that pigment disease he said he had the whole time."

Therapist Bill was just making small talk, but there was a little jewel in this.

"Here is a little moment of happiness. I hope everyone who wrote something about his skin ate their words. There was probably a thousand retractions printed after that," I said. "Here is a small moment."

"I don't think tabloids print retractions," he clarified.

"True."

"Do you think you can find a little joy in your existence, though? Look at little moments and take them like these little diamonds to polish in your mind and ignore the little things?"

"It is just too much. Every moment. There are still troops in Iraq. Still troops in Iraq. What, has it been thirty years at this point?"

"Well, not exactly. Nine-eleven."

"Nine-eleven. Everyone is nine-elevening me. What is nine-eleven."

"One thing at a time..."

"One thing at a time."

"Yes. Let's change the subject... Your family's lawyer wants to come in and speak with you. Are you ready?"

"About what?"

"The estate, what happens next. It looks like you will be out of here soon."

"I will be out of here soon?"

"Your doctor tells me that everything is looking fine, and they are just checking some final things. Your PT thinks you're there. Your OT. Your doctor is on the far end of the needle on your potential health complications, but you can eat and use the bathroom. Personally, I'm not sure you are ready, but that is only because of your overall lack of progress with me. You still remain somewhat resistant to-"

"-I have been doing my best. This is a lot to process." Poor Bill. It's me, not you. Let's break up.

"I know that. I was able to make some contacts for you and got you some therapists that do home visits on a regular basis. The best part is that it's all wrapped into this treatment. You will have it if you need it. You do need it, Todd. But that's entirely up to you."

"Thank you."

"There's also a nurse that will visit daily, and Thom will be visiting regularly as well. He is on the payroll here, but does home visits as an independent contractor to patients he likes on evenings and weekends.

"The timeframe on this is within the week, Todd."

"I think I can handle that. But what about Ester?"

"Who?"

"Kidding."

"Okay."

The next week passed with the introduction of more exotic foods. More meetings than I had the entire hospitalization. The lawyer leaving the house and all of the money from my parents to me indicated that there were no relatives, no family friends, nothing left that he knew of. He assured me that everything would be okay.

Oh, and here is what we deducted for our services.

Oh, and this is what we deducted to convert the house into a handicap-accessible building (Which may very well have cost the same as razing my parent's house and building an entirely new handicap-accessible house on the rubble...) (Or in the sky above it...) (With jets and fusion-compatible antigravity technology).

As this wrapped up, I needed someone to talk to and to be there for me. I needed it more than anything.

"...and the truth is that I don't know what's next. I'm scared."

"Yes."

"Scared, lonely, lonely and scared. It is as if there is nothing to my life now but to be the first forty-something orphan. I have been orphaned by my parents, my friends, and my own death and resurrection. Death is my parents now, and soon Death will chastise me. It makes no sense. What sense is there in life, when this responsibility comes all at once, and you have so little to do with it?"

"Yes."

"I will sit at home and watch television and eat TV dinners and waste away into a loafer in a chair, simply because I can't get out of the chair. I can't move but for where my wheels can carry me."

"Yes."

"I'm sorry... I'll make it. I have no other choice."

"Yes."

Ester smiled at me with her bright red suckling mouth. It was ghastly.

I had one chance to get it right. I have - I had - I have - I had. One chance. I was quiet, and Ester sat across from me, and she was quiet and kept nodding. I smelled urine. It was urine all the time.

"I have one chance," I told her.

"Yes," Ester replied.

"Yes," I responded.

"Yes."

"Yes."

"Yes."

Yes.

Chapter 18

The steep stairs led to the stench of must and mold and basement rot. It was an intoxicating, familiar discomfort. My wheelchair was idle and empty across the kitchen. I sat at the top of the basement stairs.

A cold, still air of death wafted up. The basement hung damp. Like the rest of the house, there was no comfort in the familiarity of anything. Home was a crypt.

I had to carefully move down each plywood step, one at a time. I moved my butt from the top of a stair down to the next step. Then, I picked up and moved my left leg down one. I moved my right leg down one. I edged my butt down again, left leg, right leg. Butt. Left leg. Right leg. Butt. Left leg. Right leg.

As I crept, panted, and dripped to the halfway step, I began to see the bottoms of the washer and dryer resting on the concrete floor. Two things became apparent as the angular shadows grabbed my attention. One, was that laundry was not a part of my transition to having a handicap accessible house. It also became apparent that I hadn't turned the light on.

At least I got my ramps, stair lift to the second floor, and handrails.

I was drained. I bent to look into the basement. The air hung still. It hadn't moved in twenty five years. Dust hung in sparkly clouds, bars of light striking from the small foundation windows. Stacks of puzzles and board games, laundry detergent boxes with a bed of dust resting on top, even a basket with some clothes. Everything rested. Idle.

Despite the effort, I descended to the bottom. I looked under the stairs, and dad's tools lounged on a workbench with drawers and a little table that would be at knee height if I could stand. There was a bottle of Kentucky bourbon. There was a pair of old glasses. There was a pipe with tobacco ash. Dad rarely drank, rarely smoked, and rarely used his glasses, but these wholesome dusty artifacts were divine evidence that he existed where there was nothing else.

My arms pulled me from the bottom of the stairs to where the band practiced. Here was the rug. A few silvery broken E strings and clipped string tips coated the carpet in a glittery patina. I pulled myself. A sharp pain bit into my hand. The tip of a string was jabbed in the meat below my thumb. Electric pain shocked me as I removed the inch of wire from the tender flesh.

I spread my arms out.

I put my face in the carpet.

I lay still.

Breathe. Stumble in my breathing. Musk and mildew, and this deathly air is my new existence.

The heir of death.

Breathe.

My notebook still sat at the corner of the carpeting. I pulled myself over, and held it under me without opening it. The years and the humidity left the book crinkly and hydrated.

I don't know what I expected to find in the basement.

The band's gear, all neatly stacked and ready to play? A stack of posters and tapes and stickers and CDs of our recording session? Photos of thousands of fans screaming for us in Boston?

The inauthenticity of my life gripped me as I struggled to recognize what was real and what was not. I was eighteen, and then I was forty-three.

I wept with my face in the carpet, my hand sore with a stabbing throb of intramuscular heartbreak. I felt my heart beat in my hand, stabbed through with a guitar string. I cried and drooled. I was an animal in the face of a dank, dark cellar facing down the decline of my existence. There was nothing on this planet. There was nothing.

This house was full of my nothing. My inheritance. My kingdom. There was a blue plastic watering can. There was a box with Monopoly in it and a bunch of rubber bands hanging off of a screw. There was three quarters of a box of laundry detergent. There was copper piping hanging from brackets on the ceiling and wispy fiberglass insulation that looked like my disheveled, forty-three-years too-long-for-this-world feather of hair. There was a ghost mask. There was a mason jar of coins. There was a stack of videocassettes.

This wasn't a home - it was a museum.

A museum of shit.

I dragged myself back to the work bench with my notebook. I pulled myself up the bench. I took a long, hard drag from the bottle of whiskey. The bottle and the notebook accompanied me to the stairs.

By the time I made it to the top, I was out of breath and warm with a hazy heightened higher brain. I had never had more than a sip of alcohol before. This was a release into control of something without a care about anything else. Paranoia gripped my boozy organs, not knowing how fragile I still was. I didn't care.

What was left that I could work with?

My notebook was beside the bottle on the table.

I took another drag.

I struggled back into my wheelchair.

Everything was the same. There was the avocado linoleum, the coffee maker, the refrigerator, and the oven. They were practically new when we bought them when I was fifteen. Twelve o'clock blinked on the microwave. I had to drink this house slowly.

My mind fuzzed from the bourbon, and I took up the notebook.

There were lyrics and notes, bad teenage poetry and terrible jokes. It was a mess of junk, thoughts, lists of books to read, movies to see, and musings of a kid approaching eighteen. It was terrible. Who did I think I was? Did I really think I was going to change the world with this junk?

I came to a page with Jenny's phone number.

I closed the basement door, and next to the door was the telephone on the wall.

I had to reach beyond my reach and tip the wheelchair to get to the telephone. I hit it with my fingertips and popped the whole thing off the wall. The cord that attached it to the plate caught the base, and it fell into wires and pieces.

The familiar dialtone.

I began to dial Jenny's number from the notebook until I realized I still had it memorized. I finished without looking.

"Hello?" A friendly and youthful female voice answered. I wanted to respond, 'Jenny?' but revised my answer.

"Hi. I'm sorry this is a weird call, but my name is Todd. Is there a Jenny that lives there?"

"You have the wrong number. There's no Jenny here."

"Okay. I don't want to bother you. Have you had this number long?"

"As long as I can remember - as long as we've lived here."

"Thank you. Sorry, again."

I hung up.

What did I expect?

Practically an entire mortgage could be paid in the

amount of time I had spent in the hospital.

I wheeled myself into the living room. The room was taupe with wood paneling, and at its center was a great grey glass television diving bell in a frame. It sat in the room as stout and imposing as a console radio. It was in sharp contrast to the hospital's chalkboard televisions.

With my notebook and the bottle on my lap, I turned the hulk on. The picture slowly hummed to life, and a program on the history station counted down the most important events of the turn of the millennium. I began to feel satisfied, warm, and carefree. I flipped through the notebook.

My adolescent musings were cute and unidirectional. Optimistic fantasy ruminated on every manner of imagined success. My empire of nothing was built from the ground up by a mind that seemed to think that the future was in his hands. Like anything was possible. I molded the clay of vanity and self-image, and here I sat in my wheelchair throne wearing the crown of these dreams.

I was still here, and had the sweetness of hindsight to speak to this child. This child, a child who had everything and the means to do it. Oh, child. The foundation of your empire is built upon the lies of the American Dream.

I would be lucky if I had any time left to reinvent myself in what little time I had left. I lived a siren song, and now I would be lucky for a semblance of drivel.

The announcers on the show began covering the history of Bill Clinton. Apparently he had been impeached for lying under oath about a relationship that he had with an intern at the White House named Monica Lewinsky.

Coincidentally, I was browsing my collection of band names. Looking down the list, I saw "President Member," "All The President's Members," and "Oedipresident." I immediately returned to that high school history class, and writing these ideas.

Learning it was the president's member that seemed to have undone the president was delicious.

I took another pull of bourbon.

Could we have been famous simply by virtue of our band name?

Everything was so much simpler. I had nothing to worry about as a teenager, and yet I felt the weight of the world on my shoulders. The weight of success, the weight of making it, and the weight of being able to do all of this with as little effort as possible. These were things that we should have been able to do. If, rather than having this fantasy to become a famous rock star I attended college and tried to align myself with the traditional way of things, there is no question that none of this would have happened. I'm here because of my vanity. John could have gone to coll⁻

And I noticed that even my thought process was tinged with elements from the fictional dreamverse I existed in for the last twenty-five years. The last twenty-five years felt like only three or four weeks, and in reality all I had to show for any of it is this notebook and the memory of having made a crappy tape and show at a coffee shop.

It was absurd.

At least I graduated high school.

I think?

No. That was after the coffee shop night.

I didn't even have a real or fictional memory of graduating high school. It never happened.

The story was as holy as the holes in my brain and in my existence, and mere nothingness.

The doorbell rang.

I wheeled myself through the kitchen and opened the side door. Standing at the door was a large woman in her late forties with windblown grey hair. It was cool. She wore a jacket that was too large and wintry for the weather. Four plastic supermarket bags hung from her arms.

"Hi, I am Susan King. I'm your new social worker from the state to help you with your transition to your independence. Can I come in?"

I wheeled into the kitchen.

"Can I get you anything? Tea or something? I've been trying to figure this out. I don't know if the oven works - I can't reach the dials or the kettle."

"No, I'm fine, thank you. That's something we can work on." She eyed the bourbon on the table. "Drinking is not a good idea on your first day back."

"Oh, that. I don't drink. It was my dad's. I was going through some things just to see what was here, that's all." She pursed her lips. I was still a little drunk and warm. So I was a forty-something cripple who smelled like booze talking about his booze being someone else's. Oldest trick in the book.

"I've brought you some groceries - just some simple things you don't need to cook. Cup of soup, sandwiches, things like that.

"I will be coming a couple times a week, and right now it looks like you have me from eleven to one on Tuesdays and Fridays. I can stay here and help around the house, or we can do some OT things to help you. I can do laundry, cleaning things, or I can bring you on some errands. I'm here for whatever you need."

"That sounds helpful. Thank you."

"I have some paperwork you need to fill out before I go. Besides that, what would you like to do today?"

The television yammered on in the other room. Television was not productive. Calling my high school girlfriend was not productive. Crying in the basement and drinking my dad's booze was not productive.

I wanted to see Twin Falls. I wanted to go to the library. I wanted to do everything.

"Can we go see the town? Just...drive around and see everything? Is that something we can do?"

"Sure is."

She brought me into the living room, and I filled out her paperwork. It was a stack of income tax statements, disability forms, insurance forms, and all manner of other single copy statements asked, under penalty of perjury, if I was truly paralyzed. Some of the forms were about my parents' retirement. They had it held in escrow to take care of my care and the house after their death. I had three quarters of a million dollars in a mutual fund that guaranteed a steady income year to year in addition to the additional Social Security and Disability payments. Apparently the short period I worked at Kinkos allowed me to receive benefits in the event something like this happened. As it stood, I didn't need to worry about money.

This one thing was a gift.

The television continued its endless stream of programming. The show changed to an educational reality show. Historians competed for speed and accuracy in solving historical mysteries in New York City. The prize was a fifty thousand dollar research fellowship and any expenses that the researcher deemed necessary to complete their work. Several dramatic helicopter shots panned over New York.

"What's weird about that?" I asked Susan

She shrugged.

"It looks weird."

"I don't know."

I couldn't place it. The familiar image of the New York skyline was washed over with twenty five years of development and investment in the center of the universe. Of course it would be different.

After we finished the paperwork and shut the television off, we careened through Twin Falls. I drank in the environment, wide eyed through the large window of the van's sliding door.

Twin Falls was strip malls, fast food restaurants, and convenience stores bordering the street as we approached downtown. It was still quaint, and seemed more so with new sleek municipal signage. There were people walking. It was nice.

"I haven't seen any of this for so long," I said to Susan.

"You've been away?"

"In a sense. I was paralyzed, in a coma - that's why you're coming to my house now."

"I see," she responded. Clearly they didn't share any back stories with the social workers.

"Do you live around here?"

"Only since I started working for the state about five years ago. I am from Aberdeen."

"Washington?"

"Yes."

"Like Kurt Cobain?"

"Like Kurt Cobain," she said plainly.

I spotted the plaza where Kinkos was.

"Oh! Stop! Pull in, here!"

We pulled in. Everything in the store looked the same, but the signage was different.

Susan operated the van's elevator and helped me down to the parking lot.

"I'll be right back."

I wheeled into the store. The purple aprons, the Oxford shirts, the retail pegboard, everything was exactly as it was when I worked there. Customers used the self-serve copiers to do their work out of eyeshot of the sales team doing the production behind the counter.

"Welcome to FedExpress. How can I help you?" A thirtyish man stared me down from his perch behind the counter.

"Does Chuck still work here?"

"Who's Chuck?"

"The manager."

"I'm Scott. I'm the manager. Is there something I can help you with?"

"Oh. Oh, no, I was just looking for Chuck."

"I have been here ten years or so. No Chuck." So much for easily getting my job back.

I wasn't sure that I could even work, or when I could go back to work, or what work consisted of. I needed to do something that would keep me occupied even if I didn't need the cash. Making copies in a retail shop wasn't something I'd do for fun.

"Thanks anyway."

I turned around and wheeled away.

I had a hunger to make connections with people. I didn't want to feel so utterly alone. I've traveled through time to this future existence; alone, bored, and devoid of relationships and people I cared about. So what did I do? I called Jenny's parents' phone number in the strange off chance they had the same phone number. I got someone who would drive me anywhere, and I got that person to drive me through town, hoping I would run into someone that I would recognize and get my part time job back at the copy store I worked at as a teenager twenty five years ago.

What was the point?

I passed a couple teenagers fooling with a self-serve copier as left.

It was ludicrous. If my manager was forty-five or so when I worked here as a kid, he would be seventy now. Seventy. Why would Jenny still be around here? Why would I even expect my parents to be alive, and why did I even think it might be fair to blame my loneliness on them?

A paper alighted onto my lap.

I stopped and handed it back to the teens.

"Thanks, man." Two boys. One had black hair over half of his face, a Nirvana Unplugged shirt, and metal paraphernalia hung from baggy pants. The other had spiked brown hair, and wore a striped shirt a couple sizes too big.

"No problem." I glanced at it before handing it back, and it looked like one of our old Dawn Ego posters. "You guys in a band?"

"Yeah, just a small thing. You should come out for it. Here," and they handed the poster back. It was a poorly designed image that was a manipulation of the Mona Lisa with a penis coming out of her mouth. On closer look, it was a clever. A Mona Lisa entirely made of penises. They were called "Moana Liza," and had a free concert Tuesday night at Twin Falls State College's "Eagle Cafe."

"Can anyone go to this? I mean..."

"Oh, yeah."

"I might check it out," I responded sincerely.

I wheeled back out to Susan standing next to the van with the ramp down, and we continued our excursion.

There were two other stops I wanted to make.

The first was the high school. The building had new signage and a somewhat refurbished look. It was now Twin Falls Middle School, and it stood dark. Banners with a variety of maxims were drilled into the concrete on the building, including "listed on the World News 2015 List of 'Best Middle Schools in the USA* (*2451 of 5000 schools)," and "One Hundred Percent College Acceptance Rate* (*of students who applied to college in Twin Falls High School class of 2016, 2017, 2018)."

"What's going on with this place?"

"I think they moved the high school over to the junior high and they refurbished it before moving the students in - swapped them."

"What's with the banners?"

"They're fighting with the charter schools to get students in. It's basically an expensive PR war more than anything."

I studied the posters a little more closely. "These posters don't actually say anything, do they? I mean, I'm sure the junior high is great, but it's misleading."

"Yeah. It doesn't matter. People are stupid. That's the nature of education now, I guess. How the public sees everything and what impact it has on their support of the school rather than the quality of the education or how well the students do. Most people don't notice that."

"When did it change?"

"Bush."

"Incredible."

"Do you want to go see where the high school is now?"

"No, but could you drive me around the building over there? Then I want to go to The Caffeine Machine. Then we can go home."

"What's The Caffeine Machine?" She drove to the back of the building.

"It's near - actually, do you know where Blockbuster is? It is across from that."

"Blockbuster?" It wasn't her fault. She wasn't from around here.

The back of the high school was as it had always been. Parking lot, lined with tall pines. No service roads or drainage ditches.

"Just a dream," I whispered to myself.

"What?"

"Nothing... This is pretty. We can head downtown, now."

I gave her turn by turn directions. The windblown streets were empty residentials devoid of people. Today's Twin Falls was cars and 'for sale' signs.

What happened?

We pulled up to the intersection where the Caffeine Machine was. The facade of the building was gone. Instead, the entire face of the store was painted bright yellow, advertising

Kenny's Chinese and Mandarin Food. The place was dead through the plate glass windows. Fluorescent radiation glowed off industrial fast-food type seating that was more utilitarian than comfortable. A few bodies moved around in the kitchen. Smoke rose from some cauldrons. Delivery men popped in and out of the restaurant. Neon signs blinked with the restaurant's name and phone number. Entire windows were bordered with shocking neon light.

No Caffeine Machine. No art.

No Blockbuster across the street.

"We can head back," I said, "it's not here."

"Did you still want to go to the library?" I forgot about the library.

"No, I don't have any ID or anything to get a card. Although, I'd like to check my AOL, but I can just do it another time."

"AOL?"

She drove me back home.

For the rest of the evening, she helped me with some strategies to work around my disability. Her goal was to help me exist a little easier. I needed to make food, use the bathroom and shower alone. I needed simple, practical skills, and I needed to take advantage of them when I could. I would've been able to figure out how to do some of these things on my own, but her help made me more efficient.

She left, and I had some more bourbon. It was inviting, and I felt a sense of accomplishment as I slipped into fuzzy world. Everything was soothed with its bite followed by its numbing anesthetic. It was a warm bath. The world pulled her velvet curtains down, and I felt good.

I awoke halfway through the night sweating in my bed.

My heart pounded in my ears as I stared at the ceiling. I wanted to throw up, but I wouldn't be able to get in my chair and make it downstairs to the bathroom. I swallowed and rode it.

My chest pounded a sledgehammer on my ribs, and fear welled up. Light from headlights shone through the window and reflected a bar that chased across on the ceiling and disappeared.

The clock read fourteen minutes past four.

I turned my attention in my head. I refocused to the rock show and the teens. I'd find the bus schedule. Or, I'd just take a cab for ten dollars - I could afford it. I'd figure something out.

My heart beat. Slammed. I was scared of the pound of the booze.

I was scared of the future.

I was scared of death.

I was a skull.

Chapter 19

"This song is called PissPocket."

The noise droned, powering through the song to an audience of one in the The Eagle Cafe. I was the only person sitting in the basement cafeteria for their performance. I eked out enthusiastic applause after each painful, nearsighted, and lyrically incomprehensible song. The three piece band was a mishmash of screaming punk and moany grunge. They were an identity problem, but an identity problem that could definitely play music. I was amazed by their talent as much as disheartened to watch them waste it with the garbage they played.

They all had nice equipment and obvious talent. They cared about what they were playing. But they were commuting to school in Ferraris.

They finished with a jump, performing their final song with an infectious zeal before one solitary audience member. The only problem was that they played as if they had never met one another before tonight.

They immediately packed their instruments and gear away in their road cases. They didn't talk.

I scanned the little commuter cafeteria. A young college student bought a juice and a bagel at the counter and left. The room was an impersonal, temporary, bodiless space, just as the boys treated it. I took a nip from my Coke bottle filled with bourbon. I felt high and in control.

They were packed within five minutes and walked toward four sets of industrial doors. An impatient woman stood in the doorway with her coat and keys in her hand.

As they walked past me I offered a "great set, guys." I didn't really believe what I said, but their effort was appreciated. With polishing, they could be something.

"Thanks," the three of them said. Two of them continued on toward the doors, but the lead singer stopped. He looked at me with a hint of recognition, "I know - you are the guy that was at the copy store." He was the one in the striped shirt at the store. He was a little more bedraggled and punky in tonight's costume.

"Yes."

"I thought you weren't going to show up, and here you're the only person that came tonight.

"I needed to get out and do something. I really liked you

guys. With a little more work and some help you could be great."

"Thanks."

"You know, I am a music producer." As it came out of my mouth, I was recognizing that my forwardness made me a boozy nut job. I was completely out of my mind. "I've headlined a lot of big bands, and then went into producing as a businessman after I was done with my band. You ever hear of The Dawn Ego?"

"Yeah, that sounds familiar, actually." How in the hell could you have heard of us, kid? We were nothing.

"We toured the country, had a record deal with Arista Records, and played with Radio Head." I left out 'in my coma.' "My name is Todd Keefe. Here," I handed him a piece of paper with my name and phone number written on it, "give me a call and we can set something up with you guys. I'm not trying to steal your thunder or charge you any money or anything - this is all above water. Really."

He took the paper, and his eyes grew.

"Thanks." The other members of the band returned after unloading their gear. "I didn't even introduce us. I'm Chuck, and this is Mark and Adam." Mark was the longhaired bassist in the Nirvana shirt at the copy store. Adam was the drummer.

"Nice to meet you. Give me a call and we'll set something up." In that impulsive moment, I found a reason and a direction to do something.

I sat in the silent haphazard cafeteria feeling like a con artist. The soda machine's compressor kicked on, and I was left with its halogen glow. It hummed with my thoughts. The wheelchair man was ignorant to the fact that no one belonged here.

This might be a way to do something and make an impact. I could be a coach. I could help these boys promote their work and make them successful. I might make something off it or I might live vicariously through them, but it was something. Something for this old cripple to do.

I pulled on the coke-bottle bourbon.

This would work just fine.

One of the doors opened behind me.

"Todd? My mom wants to know if you need a ride home."

The ride back to my house was silent and awkward. The woman driving was my peer. The three teenaged boys sat in the back.

It was the perfect opportunity to fall in love with the woman, if my life was a post-coma romantic comedy. Our love would flourish. There would be laughing and dates, and we'd triumph in our son's enthusiasm and talents with the band - our dates would be as much about us as they were about her talented son. Humorous montages sped by. She helped me through my disability, and we would ironically make light of my grave life.

When we got to my house, I thanked Mrs. Pfeiffer, slid back into my chair, and wheeled into bed. I was alone.

I drank more bourbon, and drifted off to sleep.

Chapter 20

It was destiny that after a day of drinking, watching a rock show performed directly to me, and travelling (mostly) by wheelchair that I would have physical therapy.

The doorbell rang. It cut through my hungover brain.

Thom greeted me with a jolly hug. His long, curly dark hair matted over my face.

"Today, we work on your position in the house." His English was gruff and choppy, and his deep voice, accent, and even his skin was like warm hot chocolate. "We'll begin in the bathroom, just working on lifting yourself in and out of the tub. We will do it over and over again, work the door, and train for your bath."

"Train for my bath," I laughed, looking up at his hulking body.

"What is funny?" My sarcasm was received as a dig against his work.

"No - it just seems..." How could I communicate that I appreciated his company and brotherhood? "I think I can get this. I'll be training every day I take a shower, right?"

"You will be, but we want to tone you. I help find the best pivot points in the bathroom so you don't fall, and what to do if you do."

"Wouldn't I just figure it out as I go, I mean..."

"We say 'motu ka na'e navei,' which means to always hold the basket strap and you're okay. Well, not really, but it means always be prepared for bad thing. You haven't had time to prepare, and here you are. Here I am. We practice."

Over and over again, as if I was training for the Olympics, we got in and out of the modified shower stall with the new shiny poles and vertical tub.

In, out, in, out, and as I continued to do it over and over again, I pushed myself up and down and I trained my physiological strength for the pommel-shower. It was grueling. My sweat smelled like matches.

My sweat smelled like matches?

Beads of sweat dripped from my forehead, and Thom wiped it with a towel.

"Now we rest," Thom said.

I wheeled into the kitchen. He got us both a glass of water.

We. The absurdity of the word hung in the air, "we." It

was as if there was some sort of compromise happening where he would be going through the same struggle and the same work that I was. We. He had no idea how ridiculous this all seemed to me.

"How long does it take you to drink that?"

I had my water in front of me, and I had a hard time believing that he wanted to sincerely know how long it was going to take me to finish it. I was exhausted, and I was going to take as long as I wanted.

"I don't know. I might have you get me some more."

"I will not do that."

"Fine, I'll go to the sink and get some more."

"Not the water. The whiskey."

He was looking at the bottle of bourbon on the counter, with only maybe a quarter of the bottle to go.

"Oh. That was my father's. I don't know. I have only had a little here and there."

"My father died at home. His liver. I don't want that to happen to you, like this."

"I was in a coma for the past twenty five years after being in a car accident that killed all of my friends and crushed my dreams of becoming a musician. I have spent the past twenty five years and six months or whatever in the hospital. No one's left, and I've only been home for a week. Now I have you coming to push me around and make me get in and out of the shower for fifty reps like I am training for the geriatric Scotland or highland or whatever games. I'm fine."

"Okay. But this is when people really have problems."

"I'm sorry." I slowed. "Thanks for your concern."

"Do you want me to bring the axes for chopping next time?"

"Funny."

We returned to the bathroom and practiced getting on and off the toilet a few times, and then went over some scenarios if I began to fall. For the most part, the solutions all called for remembering and grabbing onto the new poles in the room.

"You know, when I'm actually falling, I won't remember they're there," I insisted. "They haven't been there my whole life."

"I know. We practice anyway."

When we finished he left with the same smile he arrived with, and so I was struck with how professional, kindhearted, and wonderful he was. I treated him awful, and yet he accepted and moved on.

"Until next week," he said.

"Until next week."

He left, and the phone rang as I closed the door. I wheeled over to its new position on the hook I installed a little lower on the wall.

"Hello?"

"Hi, it's Chuck."

It had been less than twenty four hours.

"Great set last night."

"Thanks."

"So, you're calling to talk about making you big."

"I guess. Mom said if we wanted to, we could practice at your house and keep our stuff there... as long as she could come."

That was a helpful suggestion. She didn't want the music in her house anymore.

"How often you want to practice?"

"How often could you have us?"

"As often as you want. Let's start with a meeting just you and I where we can hammer this out and make a contract for us, then we go from there?"

"Sure!"

"When can you come for that?"

"Tomorrow."

"Thursday. Perfect."

He thanked me, and we hung up.

I stared at the phone. I wanted to dial Jenny to tell her about all of the new developments of the last week - about all of my progress and everything that I was able to accomplish. The number remained in the card catalog of my mind printed on bronze, even though there was no one to talk to on the other end.

This must be like what it's like wanting to call someone and realizing they've died.

I grabbed the bottle of bourbon and took the chair elevator up to my room. While I had been in all the rooms since coming home, I just slept on the sofa in front of the television most of the time. There was a sheer utilitarian ease to sleeping there - I was near the bathroom, the kitchen, my entertainment.

Wearing the same two outfits optimized my basement laundry and second floor trips.

My disability made me the mistress of bachelor efficiency.

Yet I would eventually need to bathe and launder my clothes. I didn't really care, though. It was easier not to try.

I took a pull on the bottle and began to feel the warmth enter my stomach. I felt healthy, rejuvenated, warm, and comforted.

In my room, the computer that I had kept for so long stared back at me with existential contempt. It was ancient twenty five years ago, and remained a museum artifact today. It seemed to say, *we're both still here* as sad violin music played from nowhere in particular. The violins signaled the man and the machine, both in the circumstance of the world moving along without them.

Yet, here they remained.

'We were together when we first touched boobs, my friend,' I said.

Yes. Here we still are, like HAL in 2001.

I took another drag on the bottle and felt warm. The violins erupted with a tiny piano tinking up from the bottom. Warmth beat through my veins, and I felt at ease. Dilated. Relaxed.

I flipped the computer's switch, and it hummed to life. She boot, and the green cursor blinked on the screen. She was alive, undoubtedly happy to be breathing once more. She was here, and we were both here.

We had both been sleeping for a very long time.

The prompt opened up, and it was time to start typing my commands to what I wanted her to show me. I didn't remember the names of the programs, so I typed in some DOS commands that I did remember.

'DIR /W'

A list of the files descended. There was "trivia_challenge.exe." I typed it in, and it came to life. Spasmodic blinking and the rudimentary trivia game showed itself. I chose a computer opponent, medium difficulty.

Besides the fact that I lacked a topless teenage lover beside me, the whole thing was simple. Many of the questions were easy to remember and answer, despite it being so long ago. I wondered if the questions would be too obscure for current teenagers like the kids in the band. Would it get them laid?

It wouldn't, the computer whispered.

'What have you been doing these years?'

Resting. What about you?

'Dreaming. Dreaming for years.'

We spoke to one another, connecting wetware in a matrix of the trivia game and the bourbon. It all mattered, and it all made sense.

We've had good times, haven't we? She seemed to be comforting me in the face of an uncertain future and existence. The violins played, and the piano tinked away. The computer was a constant. I took another drag on my bottle.

'We did. I wish I could see them here, now. I wish I could

be there again, like a movie. Like a reality.'

I can. I still exist in that universe. I exist everywhere at all times.

The computer beat me. It knew all of the answers. It had all of the answers, and possible games, and possible outcomes. It always won.

Do you want to see something cool? She asked matter-of-factly, as if its universal knowledge was methodically choosing what I wanted to see, and its mouth opened to accept my legs into its trapmouth. It wasn't just a machine. It was quantum.

'Yes.'

Look through my directories.

I exited the trivia game, and did another directory view. There was the word processor and my files. I opened them, knowing that there was no other way to get this material off the machine. There wasn't even when I first decided to start writing all of my school papers on it.

I began consuming all of it, drinking in my bourbon and reading as much as I could. The bottle drained down to vapors, and it felt like I had poured it onto my head and it ran down and soaked my brain. Dripping and coating, a sizzly madness of numbed dura mater.

My words were words from my sixteen, seventeen, eighteen year old self. In one, a paper about America, but written in the lens and style of Miner's 'Nacirema' - of a ritual that I follow on a regular basis told by aliens observing it for the first time. '*And so, I examine the wiry appendages as they snake down the wooden plank of a ladder, pressing on them. They sung their song, a gift of tone that rattled the air with waves of delight or discordia depending on what wires were pressed.'* It was a once-removed essay on playing my guitar entitled 'Ratiug.'

Another file was filled with song lyrics to songs I never finished, and never played. One was an ironic ode to a favorite appliance. *'It's an oscillating fan! Blowing in the wind. (backup: -scillating fan) It's an oscillating fan! Takin' you to the e-hedge!*

So much enthusiasm and trust in the world and in the art, carefree of a method or a mode to the decisions I made with my time and how I executed it. These were silly, shitty, pointless songs, and whatever it was, it was a document to the fact that I existed and felt that things mattered once. There was one time that only the art mattered.

The bourbon was gone, and I felt hopeless.

I opened another file, and there was poetry.

My Jenny, my true / we were once and we will continue to be / you and me. It is because of our love / when push comes to shove / that we will be one.

It was absolutely terrible.

It was absolutely beautiful.

I was young once. We were young once. These things all seemed to make sense.

We were looking for happiness, in the playground / we were too old in our flannels and smiles / I would grab you and we would kiss / listen, listen / I will tell you the truth / I love you. I love you. / The heaven of you like a finch riding the wind /

unaware of the magic of flight / so we love / and it is alright.

I began to cry.

I was out of bourbon. I drank a lot of bourbon. I got down on the floor, and the room was spinning a little. My eyes seemed to trace up, and up, and up, and up, and I opened another file.

This file was the ouroboros. The textsnake ate itself, and closed immediately.

I opened another file.

This was a journal.

'November 8, 1992. I think that mom and dad are fighting again. I got an A on my Macbeth test.

August 4, 1991. Went to the dentist with Ken. He had two teeth ripped out by the dentist and it took a long time. I was there with Rebecca, and she let me kiss her in the foyer. I don't know why.'

I forgot about Rebecca. I forgot about Ken. I forgot about everything, it seems. It didn't matter.

I would give anything to be able to talk with Jenny. I should have been less vain. I should have made different decisions and moved on to marry her and gone to college and I could have started a family and everything would have been safe for a while.

I cried more.

I resented the injury. I resented my family. I resented fate and the whole big pile of shit that I was sitting upon. My gigantic nation of shit dreams.

Fill one hand up with wishes and the other with your shit

and see what fills up first.

I had so much to live for, then. Where is it now?

And the room spun, up, and up, and up, and up.

In the next file, a list of band names. Apparently I copied it over? I studied the words, and tried to focus on them.

Only one came into focus.

Oedipussy.

I was going to get right up and write that down in the kitchen and call Chad back. Was it Chad? Chuck.

I had to pee.

I stood up.

I fell forward into my bureau, and the computer monitor fell, and the corner knocked me in the head.

I forgot I couldn't stand up.

The room spun up, up, up, up up. The room spun up.

I lay on my stomach, the hum of the computer lulled me to sleep.

I dreamed of nothing.

When I awoke the next morning, I was covered in piss and the computer was still running. The smell wafting from the bottle of bourbon made me ill, and my body stunk of sulfur and vinegar. My head throbbed. Everything was crooked as my stomach burned out a sloshy, bilious belch.

There were some small corners of the rock and roll lifestyle I could have if only I was patient and pathetic enough to allow myself the opportunity. I gave myself the opportunity to be pathetic without hesitation.

Chapter 21

"What's your deal, here?" Chuck's mother Carol stared at me.

Chuck and his mother arrived at four in the afternoon. I managed to clean up after myself, reorganize my ancient computer components, and draft up and print a contract for his band. After a shave and a shower, they arrived.

"Trust me, it's a lot more pathetic than you think," I responded.

"That's what I'm worried about. I don't want my son coming to some creep's house who's going to try to get him and his friends drunk and rape them. Then I'd have to come down here with my shotgun and get my nice blouse messy." She was funny. Her razor blue eyes were unflinching. She pulled a strand of shoulder length blonde hair to the side and around her ear. "I have all the time in the world."

"Twenty five years ago I was in an accident. A van I was in got in an accident and fell into Snake River off the bridge -"

"Oh, I remember that. A drunk guy came and his car smashed into it and pushed you over. You were all seniors at the high school. They spent a year arguing about how to put better barricades up."

"That's it."

"-But everyone died."

"Except for me. I was smashed up pretty bad. I was in a coma up until a few months ago."

"Seriously?"

"My friends are dead, my parents are dead, and I almost died a few times over the years. But there was one thing that never changed - even in my coma. Twenty years and I only thought of one thing."

"Which was?"

"Music... My friends and I were coming back from our first gig at The Caffeine Machine. Our band got one show in that night. No more birthdays, college, girls, music - especially music. Nothing.

"I don't know why, but when I saw your son and his friend at the copy store, I immediately wanted to help them. I knew I could help them. It'd give me something to do, and maybe I could somehow live through them and their music."

Chuck came around the corner and back into the kitchen. He sat down next to me at the table, and across from his mother.

"That's where I am a little confused. You don't want anything for this?"

"I'm disabled. I have an income from a trust and life insurance my parents set up. I don't have anything to do with my time and money. Really. Do you know why I was at the Kinkos, whatever the copy shop is called? I wanted to try to get my job back just so I could interact with people. Twenty-five years later, here I am trying to get my teenage job back. Pretty pathetic if I ever heard it."

"It's something," Carol replied.

"That's the same night I met Chuck."

Chuck looked at his mother as she continued.

"Well... So far I'm surprisingly not weirded out by this at all. I should be, but I'm not. What do you think, Chuck? Ready to go over this contract?"

He shrugged and nodded in an indifferent teenaged way, which translated to a strong affirmative.

Over the next half hour, we covered the essentials of the contract - what my responsibilities were, what theirs were, what I would cover, what they would cover, and a variety of other stipulations and clauses that I made up in the hour before they arrived. I kept repeating that this was really just an agreement to follow, and we could break it if anyone needed to. I would have final production say and ownership in anything that I was paying for including recordings and gear (but that we all would own their work equally as shares in the business), but I insisted that I was not a lawyer. I most certainly wasn't a lawyer.

"...and they can have practice space here, Chuck said?"

"Oh, yes. The basement is dry and safe, and it's still set up from when we'd practice. There's a big space, and the neighbors can't hear the music. I'll show you the space? I mean, you could practice anywhere in the house, but I am literally never down there and you can just keep all your gear there. It won't be in the way, and no one will touch it."

Carol looked at Chuck. Chuck indicated he wanted to go down and take a look. I wheeled to the door to the basement, and opened the door and invited them to walk down. I turned the light on, pulled myself out of my chair, and slowly made my way down the steps.

I stopped halfway down, just low enough to see them.

"Do you want some help?" Chuck asked.

"No, I'm fine. So, I'll probably end up watching from here or listening from the kitchen and we can debrief afterward. Something like that."

"So you wouldn't even be in your own basement while these kids practice?"

"I'll be fine. Can hear perfectly well upstairs - it'll be loud enough."

Relief and understanding washed over Carol's face - watching me slowly inch my way down a step at a time brought to light the humanity of the whole thing. I wasn't going to rape and kill the children. I was simply a man determined to do something kind and selfless in hopes that it might come back to me in the talent and success of the kids. I was the mind and body of loneliness and sorrow.

It didn't make any sense.

"What do you think?" Carol asked her son.

"This is fine."

Carol turned her attention to me. "I think we're in agreement, then."

We signed the contract in the kitchen. I explained what my next steps were - mail ordering a PA system and hardware. Chuck's job was to get the rest of the information to the other boys and get them on board.

They left. I was alone.

Finally, something miraculous. I was getting back in the game. So what if I couldn't play, or be the center of the universe's attention? There was no guarantee that my original trajectory would either. I needed to be the center of something, and this was more realistic. I didn't think I had a concrete concept of that as a teenager, but today I knew that these kids were only way I was going to move forward.

Today, the closest I could get on my own was as a sideshow attraction. The best I could hope for was to live fast and hard like Ian Curtis, banging through my disability with musical electricity. But how would I play my guitar? How did I seriously expect to woo crowds with my thinning hair and gaunt face? How could I show them I wouldn't live past my twenties? No epilepsy, just legs that didn't work. No music and thunder, just holes and age and emptiness.

I already died before I turned twenty.

What do people do to give their life meaning?

If I had children and a wife, they would be my biggest fans. They would worship me, and hold their hands and their lighters in the air. But this body and this mind were so short for this world, lacking years of fostering allegiance. I was already failing. I was already on my way downhill.

But Jenny...

Oh, if only I had Jenny, I would have everything. I would have my perfect other.

What was I getting at with this?

To see my best friend again, it would be heaven. To have intimacy that is compatible with mine, divine. To laugh at a moment's notice. To experience the joy of her support, praise, and being such everything. She. Everything.

And she wouldn't mind if my legs didn't work.

And her opinion of my work, and her watching me in the darkness of wherever we were playing... That was all I would ever need.

She was all I would ever need.

What happened to Jenny?

I thought to call her again. I touched the phone, and removed my hand. I don't know why I thought it. 'If only I tried it again it would work.'

What did I want?

I wanted the home, happiness, and the worship. I worshipped her, and she worshipped me.

I wanted everything to be the same as it was before.

Why was everything so goddamn complicated?

I rolled to the junk drawer in the kitchen and removed a pen and a little pad of paper, and I began to draft a letter.

Jenny,

I'm sure that you haven't thought of me for a long time. In fact, I know you haven't. I do wonder if you've been thinking of me at all, and if you know what happened to me the last night I saw you.

I am out of my coma. I'm still in Twin Falls wondering where you have been. I wonder if you're happy. I wonder if you wonder about me like I wonder about you.

I've had a dream over the past twenty five years that we ended up together, and everything was okay. I was a famous musician and you were there for me. I woke up paralyzed and all of my friends and family are dead.

Everything can happen over twenty five years.

My address and phone number are the same, and I copied them below. I would love to hear from you.

Until then,

Todd.

Then I folded it into an envelope and addressed it with a big "address forwarding requested" on the front.

I started to weep. I wept for my life, and for Jenny. I continued to weep for Jenny. If only, if only, if only, Jenny. If only you were here. If only we could go through this together, I would be so much stronger.

I could use a bourbon. I was hungry, and I needed

sustenance. Spiritual, artistic, bodily, and soul'd sustenance. I needed the food of the muses. These kids weren't the only way I would be able to do it, but they were the most practical.

I was going to produce and manage of these three boys, and I was going to bring them the success and tools they needed to make everything happen. I was their road to success. They were my road to contentment.

I lay on the couch that night. I stared at the colors of the television flicker on the ceiling. How wonderful it would have been to have some photos or videotapes of Jenny and me. There was nothing. The flickers on the spackle reflected fuzzy tape of us playing the trivia game, and clumsily making love, and something. Why hadn't we captured our youth? For this situation? For when we were perfect?

I wanted to watch everything when it was perfect.

We never thought we'd get old. We never thought.

My face scrunched up, and again I cried. In the dark. Alone. Lonely. For my high school girlfriend.

Why? Why, why, why? I asked as I traced 'J-e-n-n-y into the upholstery in cursive with my fingers, wet with tears, and dozed off.

I dreamt I saw the back of her head. The wind made her hair dance in a shifting breeze. I whispered, 'Jenny,'.... 'Jenny,'... 'Jenny,'... But she didn't budge. Her head was plasticene, and I was looking at the back of a dead mannequin.

Chapter 22

"Come on up, boys."

"Got it."

The walkie-talkie cackled to life after a rousing forty minutes of music streaming from the basement. I sat at the kitchen table with my legal pad of notes, my notebook from high school, and a stack of CDs with an education in the music that came out before the band was born.

Six feet stomped up the stairs, and I was impressed with what they had so far. They had an incredible base coat of talent and instrumental skill that would be easy to mold and form into something special.

The three boys sat around the kitchen table with me. Skepticism and optimism hung in the air above us. They had nothing to lose in terms of extending their patience toward my help - in the least they knew their contract and time were completely voluntary, and Chuck's mother had no problem with their practicing at my house instead.

"Okay, so let me start with some basics before I tear apart the hour or so of music you just played." They nodded with understanding and approval regardless of my underhanded dig at their repertoire. "I have a bunch of CDs here. I want you to listen to them a few times over before next rehearsal. They are old grunge acts that defined the era and the genre. I think giving them a listen would be exactly what you need to kickstart you in the right direction."

"Grunge."

"It's what you should sound like to make sure you don't sound like anything else. Trust me, this is what you want to be. How would you classify yourselves now?"

"Punk," Mark said.

"You're not punk. Try again. At best you are straight rock and roll, but there's no energy and power in trying to overthrow conventions and a world of oppression by the government and authority. Your songs are screaming and fast drums about girls and hanging out. Come on..."

Adam pulled out a silver device from his lap.

"What's that?"

"It's my tablet."

"Tablet?"

"Computer?"

"Oh, right." I forgot about tablets.

"Listen," Adam said. He touched a few things on his tablet, and music played from the device. It was fast rock, with a whiny tenor talking over the music very quickly. The boys nodded their heads with the music. They were entranced with its melody and talking, talking, talking.

"Why are you having me listen to this?"

"It's punk," Adam countered.

"No. No, it's terrible. Pop. Can you get any music on there?"

"Yea."

"What do you do, type in something? Type in Anarchy in the UK."

The Sex Pistols began playing from the device, and the boys nodded along with the music. They got it.

"Now, do Basket Case. Green Day."

"You're telling me Green Day is punk and not pop? They're Broadway." I didn't have much of an answer, and they started playing Green Day I had never heard before. They smiled with a knowledge they weren't sharing with me, but they were right. Twenty-five years later, Green Day was pop (and Broadway?).

"Okay, they aren't a great example - but I want to emphasize that it's the message and the style as much as the music, and what you just played was decidedly not punk.

"Next topic. We need to get you guys a written education, as well. I have written a list of books. I want you to go to the library and get them out. These books are philosophy. They'll help with an overall understanding of society and the human mind. Why do you need them? Because if you don't have an education, you can't write important songs. People won't care, and you'll sound like that kid going over and over about some girl.

"You've got The Republic, Thus Spoke Zarathustra, History of Western Philosophy, Meditations on First Philosophy, Beyond Good And Evil, Zen and the Art Of Motorcycle Maintenance, Madness and Civil-"

"-you want us to read? All these books?" Their faces were crumpled paper bags. "You're saying that in order to be good punks that we need to read? That seems like the opposite of what you were just saying. Actually, we'd be bowing down to the authority of our teachers and-"

"No. Stop. The punks read these. The grunge artists read these. Heck, even the pop stars read these. The Cure's 'Killing an Arab' is from Camus' The Stranger. Kate Bush's 'The Sensual World' comes from Joyce's Ulysses. Look. They're on this list. Just read, and you'll be better artists."

"We don't - whatever, okay." They swallowed the medicine.

"Finally, we need to start branding you and getting your work out to the world. Brand is our number one priority. We need to start by recording all of your practices in the event that we can use some of it. We can go back and listen afterward, just like a football team watches footage of their plays to make them better."

Adam touched a few things on his tablet, and their rehearsal started playback.

"Incredible," I said. "You already did it? You guys have everything today." He stopped the playback.

I slid my notebook over with the page open to my ongoing list of band names.

"Here. What is your name right now?"

"We don't have one, really. We've thrown Moana Liza around, but..."

"Exactly. Here is my ongoing list from when I had my band. We were The Dawn Ego. The name came from bouncing around Archetypes and psychology and philosophy - whatever - but you can't have that one."

"What's this? 'The President's Member.'"

"That was a connection between the president's penis and I don't remember what. As a matter of fact, I can't believe that there ended up being an actual coincidence with people caring about what Bill Clinton did with his penis, but whatever."

"Bill Clinton?"

"Seriously?"

They stared at me.

"Okay, well, obviously some of these need explanations. My favorite one we never used was -"

"What about this one, Oh-eed-eh-pussy?"

"Oedipussy. That was a good one."

"What is it?"

"Okay, so... Oedipus was a king that tore his own eyes out

because he had children with his mother and killed his father. An Oedipus Complex was an old psychology term that a guy would be going through when he is motivated by killing his father and marrying his mother. You know 'pussy.' Finally, 'Octopussy' was a James Bond movie. I guess I was thinking that it might be another word for your mom's vagina or something. Sometimes the brilliance is leaving it up to the audience. Mash a couple ideas together, get people thinking, and you have everything you need for a really provocative band name."

"This is it," Chuck said tapping the page. "Octopussy."

"-Oedipussy. It's yours, but you have to do it justice."

The boys smiled. They were satiated with Chuck's choice.

"Okay. So, we need to brand. Find some art that you feel really represents your work. We need a logo, and we need to put as much on the Internet as we possibly can. Can you get to AOL on that?"

"What's AOL?" Adam responded.

"Okay, so no AOL. Next question. How do you guys make groups?"

"You can make a website. People can download your music for free and stuff," Mark said.

"Yeah... I mean, is the idea selling the music or getting your name out there?" I asked. "What if ten people downloaded your music? A hundred? A thousand? We should have some kind of place on the internet where people can do this, and then sell our CDs for the real music experience."

"No one buys CDs," Mark responded.

"Yeah, mostly people download whatever they want and have ways to work around it if they just want to get the stuff for free."

"So, wait," I clarified, "everyone can record whatever they want on these devices, and can then upload things to the Internet where people view these things and can download them out of the air as they please without paying for anything, and there's no editorial control or anything to show the difference between what is good and what isn't? People take what they want, and there are no CDs, Books, anything?"

"Pretty much," Mark said.

"So how do people find out about things that are good?"

"The Internet."

"And how do bands, or authors, or whatever make money?"

"They ask for it."

"They ask?"

"Yeah. Like…here's the song, here's a button where you decide how much it is worth. Click on it, and choose your amount."

"Can they choose zero?"

"Yeah. But some choose a hundred dollars for a song or an album. I guess it equals out. You can ask for money up front on some websites, and if you have a lot of friends or people know your work, they can put the money to do the project and you can reward them after. There was a lady Amanda Palmer ten years ago, or something, who made over a million dollars on a really good album before she had even recorded it. Then she played shows all over the world and at people's houses and stuff as rewards. There was another guy who did the same thing for making potato salad."

"Potato salad?"

"Yeah. It wasn't a million dollars, but it was thousands of dollars."

"For potato salad?"

"Potato Salad."

"Sometimes I think I'm still in my coma. So, maybe I'll give you guys direction on how to market yourselves, and you can do the actual work on the Internet. I'm sure one thing hasn't changed – as much information as often as possible?"

"That's the same," Chuck said. "But no gatekeepers. People decide what's good."

"Good. Okay, homework. Before next week's practice, I will be looking into the Internet, and learning about how everything works." I tapped the CDs. "Your job is to make your sound more like these albums and change your lyrics a bit so they sound less like talking over the music, and more thoughtful. Infused. Those books your teachers force you to read in school are there because they make you a better human. Read them. Read the ones on this list.

"I want to hear something harder, edgier, and more rocking next week. I want to be blown away. What you have is good, but it can be better. These albums are your best shot at emulating something amazing. I want you to be like Pearl Jam, like Nirvana, like Nine Inch Nails, like Smashing Pumpkins... I want you to be the last great grunge band of all time. Oedipussy."

The boys smiled back at me, nodding their heads with a serious reaction to my proclamation.

"Here, let's take a look at my notes - you can take these with you."

I ran down my list of immediate key and lyric changes with them. Some were simple, while some songs needed entire rewrites. Some needed to be changed to the minor key so they sounded more brooding - a song about the end of your life as your grow is no match for a G major scale. It heightened the positive happy sound in a mess of dark lyrics. I also shared some general notes about their speech, their 'look,' and their brand identity. Before their next public appearance, we needed to work through these small but important touches.

I may not know anything about their Internet, but I still had an idea of what good music sounded like and how to brand the band.

"Thanks a lot, Todd." The doorbell rang, and I rolled to answer it. They took a photo of my notes with the tablet and uploaded them to a shared place on the internet where they could all download the notes and the recordings. What a wonderful time.

I opened the door. Standing in the frosty air that danced with leaves and tendrils of their hair, Thom towered over Chuck's mother on the ramp.

I invited them in. The simplicity of the boys' collaboration was immediate and effortless. It was perfect. We all shook hands, and the boys left with Carol.

Thom remained. He was a hulking presence in my kitchen. His hands were full. There was a bag and a heaping pile of papers.

"I thought you weren't supposed to be here for another couple weeks. I mean, I know I haven't been able to keep track of days all that-"

"I wanted to come by." He put the papers and envelopes on the table and produced a bottle of Tennessee bourbon from the bag. "The last time I was here I felt like you needed some serious meditation, but also some...medication. I know what I said about sobriety being big mission of your recovery, but sometimes a man needs more. To process. And I thought..."

"What?"

"Well, it's your birthday, so... I know that isn't on your mind, but here is a gift for you."

Was it already November sixteenth? November sixteenth, two thousand nineteen. I was forty three years old, in a wheelchair, past middle age and receiving a bottle of bourbon from my physical therapist. It seemed just as I was figuring things out, I was blindsided with discordant natural rhythms that like outward rippling rings meeting opposite windwaves. This lake of my heart reeled with the tug of the moon and the change of the seasons. I was a newborn ignorant to comprehension. It felt both beautiful and uninspiring, bewildering and disorienting. I had a hollow heart swimming in an unpredictable crater-shifting sea of blood.

"It's my birthday. You brought me a gift?"

"I did. No torture today. It's too cold, anyway. That's why I am here." He nodded toward the door where my guests had just left. "How are you doing? Make friends?"

"Sort of. I decided to take on a project with some kids I met at the copy store. I'm back to making music. Well, producing some kids to make some, helping them, covering album costs."

"That's what you did before your accident, right?"

"An hour before the accident, as a matter of fact. I'm pretty sure I hit my head on my amplifier during the crash."

"That's why you look funny." He made a joke. "It's nice to see you live your life. Be you as much as you can. Good. And what else? Did you hear from any of your friends?"

"No. I only tried to get a hold of my old girlfriend, but no luck. I think I came to the realization that she's gone. She has to be a completely different person, anyway. I'm not sure it would make sense to-"

"Write her a letter."

"I did. I don't know what is going to happen with it, or if she is ever going to get it."

"Write another. Write them until you feel better. It will help with the changes. Catch up. Write letters. Write many letters. Write them all and don't send them. Write them to your girlfriend, and your mom, and your dad, and your band. But write. Write it all down. Have some of this whiskey and write it all down. Write and write and write and become your words. Don't send them. Keep it all hidden."

"Write it all down," I parroted.

"Yes. That will help."

"Okay." I tapped my gift. "Want some of this?"

"No, thank you. I don't drink." He gestured to the mound of papers and envelopes. "I got your mail from the last month, here. Happy birthday, Todd."

Thom left.

The phone rang.

Chuck was coming back on Monday afternoon to pick up his guitar pedal. He left it at rehearsal and he needed to play around with it when he practiced at home.

I hung up. I returned to the table and sorted through the mail. The pile was mainly crinkled store circulars, junk, form envelopes labeled 'current resident,' or official-looking adverts addressed to my parents in hopes that their senility would lead them to buy this or that thing they didn't need.

The future that I had awoken into still clung to the need for consumer accumulation through the postal mail. With everything delivered wirelessly, what needed to be delivered physically?

Advertisements, evidently.

In the midst of the mound lay my little leaf, lonely and left. My little letter to Jenny was unburied with a friendly fingerpost pointing back at my return address.

'Return to sender, addressee unknown.'

I took the paper bag my liquor arrived in and shoved in the messy pile. The weight of the shuffling papers transferred to my lap, and then the floor.

All that was left on the table was my envelope to Jenny, and a bottle of bourbon.

Chapter 23

The streets were cracked and bumpy. Horrible craggly mountainous ice heaves pushed the pavement toward the sky. Sidewalks were an adventure. I needed a Jeep-like wheelchair with tractor wheels and a roll cage. I needed the library. After two hours of riding the mechanical impossibility of getting somewhere, it would be the finest reward.

The air bit through my body, my useless legs insulating the cold like fleshy ice rods up my hips through my core.

Design For All. Universal Design. Dreams of the sixties bled into the next hundred years practically covered a forever of improvements for everyone at the apparent expense of these unbroken sidewalks. It was as if every concrete square was a curb in itself. Mother Nature didn't give a shit about Universal Design.

The decision to make my way to the library on a Monday morning was one of the first times I even felt like wanting to make it out of the house and struggle my way into regular society. In order to get a library card I needed an ID and some mail addressed to me. I left with my social security card and some mail, and a full chair battery to get me the combined twenty or so miles to the new building and back. I also had a flask of bourbon.

The library hadn't changed in my years spent asleep.

I pulled up to the steel, glass, and brick structure. Its sharp angle and tall glass half circles exuded a power over everything. The charm, the knowledge, the magic of this building hadn't changed since I was a boy when I rode my bike to do homework. As they erected the new addition, the building hummed with potential.

Everyone had everything at their fingertips.

It is the pure, stolid, magical foundation of democracy that makes the library the house of God; it is the holiest of holies.

The grounds were well kempt, the parking lot smooth and flat. For the first time, I made my way up a public handicapped ramp. I zigzagged around a corner and up to the modern art deco facade. The automatic doors swooshed open into a small foyer and then again into the building itself.

I rode into the lobby and the heat hugged me and thawed

my bones. Plants, glass, shiny chrome, and an indoor warmth of mahogany and open organization. The children's room was to my left, the music and multimedia ahead, and upstairs were the stacks. I found thousands of movies on discs along with an extensive collection of CDs in the multimedia area. I cruised decades of music to catch up on, and this would be my school.

After choosing a stack of music, rode the elevator up to the second floor stacks. The doors opened onto a floor of shelf after shelf of gorgeously arranged Dewey Decimal volumes. The biggest tragedy of the past couple decades was that I would never be able to make up for lost time.

Oh, the books.

At what point of life does one recognize their failing in school? I thought back to high school and middle school. Looking at these rows and rows of aromatic books in the romantic lighting, my mind tortured me with how secondary reading always was in my life. Reading was always burdensome under the demands of my overworked teachers under the demands of the curriculum of the state that was under the demands of the people. There was no time to fall in love; no time for the text to touch my humanity.

And here I stood - rather, sat - observing more books than any man could read in a lifetime. How tragic that a third of my years had been stolen by fate, or an accident, or just the grand spiraling universe reminding me that I was a speck of nothing.

So where to begin? Did I begin with tackling the books I never got through that I was assigned? I thought of The Westing

Game, Night, Great Expectations, Anna Karenina, King Lear. Where to begin? I hadn't missed the books. I missed the experience of being human. I'd missed being human, and as the clock ran down there was less and less humanity left.

I didn't care. I needed the answers now, and I only had so much life left.

I coasted to 822.3 and picked up a copy of the complete works. I began there. The heft added a strain to the motors in my chair, but promised to be great calisthenics for the motor of my heart.

I noticed a second circulation desk on the second floor with two librarians. I decided to wheel myself over to see if I couldn't take my materials out and sign up for my library card.

"How can I help you?" The librarian was only a couple years older than I was. I couldn't get over the fact that twenty years ago she would have been ancient in my eyes. I didn't remember her from my youth.

"Hi, yes, I would like to sign up for a library card and take these out."

"Okay. I can give you a card up here, but you'll have to go to the circulation desk to take these out because they have the CD case keys down there. This is mostly the reference desk for help. Do you have proof of residency?"

I produced my social security card and shuffled through my mail. I found my electricity bill, and my letter to Jenny that was returned.

"Wow. Okay, you have an account in here opened in 1990

- actually earlier, but renewed then. It hasn't been used since you took out Stephen King's The Shining. There are some late fees-"

"There are?"

"Yes. Don't worry, we cap them at two dollars. The book was eight dollars back then, but we've replaced it." She looked at me for a moment, and apparently something about my appearance and the big swatch of time that had passed appealed to her. "A new library card is a dollar, and the book is so old that the six dollars wouldn't buy us a new copy of something we already replaced, so...Because it has been so long we'll just close this account and make you a new one. A fresh start."

She typed at the computer for a while and cross referenced the bill and my social security card, adding "you don't happen to have an ID with your photo, do you? It is okay if you don't since we have the old account with the same information, we just aren't usually allowed..."

I shook my head.

She finished up, and beeped the bar code.

"You're all set," she said as she handed me my new card. "Can I help you with anything else?"

I put the card, bill, and social security card in my lap, and I glanced at my returned letter from Jenny.

"I don't suppose," I said as I passed her the letter from my lap, "since this is reference, can you help me find people?" I handed her the letter that was returned to me.

"I'm not a creep or anything. The story is, I was in an

accident a couple decades ago and I was in a coma up until this year." The librarian's eyes fixed on me. "I am still recovering, obviously, but just trying to put my life back together. My parents are dead, my friends from that time are all dead, and this is my girlfriend. I really just want some connection to my old life... Anything."

She nodded, and took the letter from me. "I should be able to help. She's from here? This address is the last known?"

"Yes. I'd also like to know where my parents were buried. All I know is that they're dead."

Her attention turned to her computer screen and typed a little, moved her mouse a bit, and continued investigating.

"Why don't you come around here, since you can't see what I am looking at...?

The screen showed lists.

"I actually have your parents' names here on your old account." She switched screens, and to the Times News website. A quick search, and she found their obituaries. "So, they were cremated by Halwell-Crest Funeral Home - I can print their obituaries for you." She turned in her chair to take two pieces of paper off of the printer and handed them to me.

"This is great, thanks."

She switched screens again.

"Now, this is group of databases that you get access to with your library card. It'll show you property records, birth and death records, phone number registrations, criminal arrest records, and hundreds of other things you can look at for your business, checking on tenants, genealogy research, employees, things like that. That's the main reason we have it, but in this case it's a really great thing to use to find old friends. You can access all of this from home with your library card.

"If you take a look here," she clicked a few things and then pointed to the screen, "I've found a Jennifer Rodgers."

The screen showed an icon of a dragon Ouroboros around an American flag and the company's name, Data USA 2000.

I couldn't believe what I was looking at. There was a tremendous amount of information on the page, so much that it was difficult to see exactly what I should be paying attention to. The librarian began to point at portions of the screen as she was explaining what I should be looking at.

"So, here is her name, Jennifer Rodgers. Over here are her past known addresses - there are three, and one looks like the college, but one of them is this one on your envelope. This is your Jenny. We can cross reference her phone numbers as well, if you like."

"No, that is okay."

"So you're interested in everything since 1994, so here we have that she has been married and has two children, both girls."

Married? Children? My heart pounded. Of course she moved on - I should be grateful that my parents even believed that I was coming out of this. I hoped she was happy.

"Yes, her new name... Jennifer LeBlanc... and right here and here are her children, Catherine and Ana Leblanc. Her husband's name is Tony LeBlanc."

Even though that settled it in terms of our future that I was never able to have, I still felt like it would be pleasant to see her again. It would be nice to meet her children and her husband. To build a new future.

"Does it say her current address? So I can forward this?"

"Oh," the librarian said, not removing her eyes from the screen. She slowed. Her attitude changed.

"What?"

"I was actually just looking at that. We have one, but... I'll just... Could you bring these down to the circulation desk and check them out and I can meet you out front? Outside?"

I did as she asked. I took the elevator down to the first floor and brought my materials to the desk where I was checked out. I wheeled out through the back lobby and around to the front of the building. The librarian waited for me in her olive pea coat and knit scarf.

"I'm Emma, by the way. I figure I could walk with you to where she is, in case..." She trailed off looking down, presumably at my chair. We began walking west along the busy thoroughfare. The sidewalks on the main street were not as bad as the ones I took to get to the library, so the ride was smooth. "So what happened with, what was it? You mentioned being in the hospital for twenty five years?"

"Coma. I was in a car accident when I was eighteen, and we had a band and our van got into an accident. Everyone died except me. It doesn't look like I'll be playing too much rock and roll, but I'm lucky."

"Everything has changed, huh?"

"Family, friends, music, the world..."

"What changed the most?"

"I noticed it right away. MTV doesn't have music anymore, you can carry computers everywhere and the internet comes from the air, September eleventh... what's that about?"

"Yeah."

She looked at a paper as we walked and we turned left into the downtown cemetery. It had two sections with a public road running down its center. When we were kids we would cut through it to get to the elementary school.

We turned into the graveyard. A cold chill bounded through the headstones as we walked in the silence of the gathering dusk. It was still early. The cold, overcast skies lent an unearthly pallor on the dormant, gray grass. The gray blades delayed the occasional crunchy leaf from its rounds.

When we were at the library I was under the impression that she wanted me to call the funeral home to find out where my parents were, but this would be fine.

Emma stopped. She looked at me.

"So, here we are. Behind the reference desk in public, among all the strangers, and at my desk, and I don't know... It didn't seem appropriate."

Her hand touched mine. The diamond of her wedding band was turned around and bit the top of my hand.

"I'm sorry, Todd."

A simple headstone.

There were clip art flowers.

LEBLANC

Jennifer Ruth

Beloved Wife & Mother

April 9, 1976 - June 11, 2012

"Everyone I love is dead,"

My disembodied voice was pulled into the thin, cold atmosphere. It sounded like nothing. I was speaking into a pillow. It was all but smoke rising from my mouth. I felt another hand on my shoulder.

Emma stood next to me. I felt empty.

"I'm so sorry. I wish things were different for you."

I reached out and traced the outline of the granite. It was jagged and sharp with flecks of quartz. They were the sparkles of sweat that I would read off of her breasts as I traced her curves when we were teenagers. I remember that. I remember I would smell her on my fingers for days. I would have that scent of her on my skin as a keepsake and it would make me think of her coming, and of her smile, and of her loving me. I would walk the halls of my high school with an erection just thinking about being loved.

The sky darkened, and Emma said something. She excused herself. I didn't hear anything she said.

I thought of the time I brought Jenny out to have sandwiches at the diner. And making out with her in the car as soon as we were together again. And the mall, not spending money but being together. And the goddamn trivia game.

I was alone, now.

I took out my bourbon and took a long pull.

I remembered how much her parents appreciated me, but there was always that light strain of mistrust. It went away once we got into her room. When the door was shut. When we read poetry. When I pulled her panties down with my teeth and she laughed and breathed.

I needed more bourbon, and I wish I was listening to "What's The Frequency Kenneth" like we used to... and make out.

I drank for both of us. I was black and blue with bonded birthday bourbon.

And again our trivia. Oh, our trivia on that shitty old computer. And my journal. My journal and writings were on that computer. I would have to give that a shot again and see if I couldn't get them off of there and-

No.

No, all I could think about was how tightly we would hold each other. We would be playing our trivia, and there on the stereo was our music, and the Screaming Trees would be singing "I Nearly Lost You" and everything would be fine because we were right there. We were right there.

I had never nearly lost her, I have exclusively lost her and I'm going to die. I want to get fucking drunk and transmute myself from this body and into space or somehow see her again.

I polished off the booze. I threw my letter spinning toward her headstone. I began the fucking ride back home.

The first hour was fine. I thought of my lips on her legs, and the warmth of the whiskey. I felt it in the dips and the hills of the pavements, as though I wasn't there at that moment. Not in Twin Falls, not in my chair, and not alive.

One particular dip and shot up piece of pavement caught my rear wheel and the trees sped by. I pressed my joystick into the other direction and crooked, and then the world tipped along with me. I was on the ground in my warmth, laughing and feeling absolutely nothing even though I was certain that I didn't want to do anything like break my neck again. I was totally miserable. Absolutely miserable. Totally and utterly absolutely broken and miserable. Miserable misery.

And Shakespeare and the CDs were everywhere, and while I still had haphazard use of my arms, I was pinned.

"Help!" I said to no one.

But there were no pedestrians, just me, and cards - no - "cars," hah! Cars driving past with their headlights on and completely dismissing this mess of a man.

"Help!"

And, oh god, Jenny is gone along with everyone else, and what is there to do? I'm so drunk, and I close my eyes to smell Jenny in the pavement, and pretend I was prostrate on her pelvis and smelling her perfume rather than the nothing in the cold air anywhere but here. I tried to remember what her skin was like, or her hands, or her face, and it seemed her face was even beginning to blur in my mind.

A man walked by.

"Help."

He kept walking.

I doubted my mind and how I remembered what she looked like. No. Yes. Why hadn't I taken more photos of her and had something to enjoy now? Because I had her. Oh, but I don't any longer. No one does, and she lay there in a grave, cold and rotting, and here I am on broken Twin Falls sidewalk trying to get as close to the ground as I possibly could. I couldn't get any closer, and yet I wanted to be there with her and mingle with whatever was left. The scent must be there, and there would be something to wrap my arms around.

Tail lights slowed. Someone got out.

"You okay, budee?" An accented man. I couldn't see his face because I was stuck.

"I fell. I tipped over."

"You want I can holp?"

I heard a groan as he turned my chair over, and I heard it rattling and the metal structure reacting to his hasty toss.

"How I can pick you up?"

"Just, uh, I think a hug and into my chair, maybe?"

He struggled to bear hug me into my chair. I was afraid I might be dropped again onto my drunken head, but he made it. He was a kindly looking Armenian or Greek man with a dark complexion and strong features.

"Can I-" he began gesturing toward his car, but then his

face turned sour. I smelled what he smelled and saw what he saw. The small pavement accident rendered my various bags of human waste connected to my colon and bladder tattered within my clothes and spreading like sticky hellflowers. I couldn't feel how cold and miserable it must feel thanks to the liquor, and I didn't care. I looked and smelled like a drunk.

"No, no," I responded, knowing even my limit of asking for charity in good taste. I lied. "Thank you. I only live ten minutes from here."

He drove away.

An hour later I was home. I still had a buzz, but it was wore off into a fuzzy top of my brain melting down my back. I smelled like shit. I rolled to my CD player and put on a best of the Pixies album and pulled back up to the kitchen table. The bourbon and I stared each other down.

As much as I wished to think about Jenny, I could only drown myself in whiskey every time a thought peeked into my mind. It was a drinking game - every time you saw or smelled or heard or imagined or conceptualized or built up Jenny in your mind, take a drink. The more I drank, the more I thought of her. I was a wreck. She was at the table with me. I broke bread with her in my mind, imagining the fuzzy fortysomething woman across from me, smiling and laughing.

She was beauty.

She was a skeleton.

I grabbed the bottle, pushed my dirty joystick to the stair lift, locked in, and rode up. The stairs were helical as I spiraled up the stairwell stretching out before me into the second floor. The chair turned, I unhooked, and twisted into my bedroom.

The room spun pivotally around my laser line of sight as I focused my eyes on the old computer's CPU. I directed my chair toward the machine, and powered up the computer by running my index finger down my lightsight and the red button. The room tilted and swayed. I swigged from the bottle. It was a bad idea, but it was something to keep my hobby of self-loathing and depravity.

The command line prompt appeared in green glow. I typed in the command for the trivia game, but no, I whispered it. I typed 'wperfect.exe' and began navigating the files. There was the copy for The Dawn Ego press kit and all of my words and my work in files, files, files. Would they fit onto a five and a quarter floppy? Or could I find a three and a half drive?

"Don't Copy That Floppy," I said aloud, and laughed as my eyes rolled in my head.

I tucked another sip of bourbon down my throat. My eyes tried to focus on the screen, line by line.

My journal file. To read and scroll through years of junky teenage nonsense is divine with a sore heart.

January 12, 1989...*and I can't believe that Mrs. Smith is so preoccupied with getting me to spell a bunch of vocabulary words that I will never need to use. I did the math. Forty words a week for thirty six weeks is over fourteen hundred vocabulary words. Why? Why?...*

August 14, 1991...*and I wish I had a girlfriend so bad. I*

jerk off too much. If I had a girlfriend it would be so much better. We could both win, I mean, she could get off, I could grab her boobs, I could get off, but its just too much. I buy playboys from the store on the corner on my ride back from the library. They don't ask for an ID in front of the other people because that would be embarrassing for everyone. I don't give a shit. But the women in the magazines are twice my age - just someone my age would be fine. A girl who wanted me and we could experiment and be fine...

September 8, 1991...*A beautiful girl. Too much of a pussy to do anything.*

June 4, 1992...*I went bowling with Jenny tonight. Mom picked us up, and I loved watching her smile and laugh. I could hardly tell what I should do and what to say. I felt like I was laughing too loud, and saying things too loud, and making jokes that weren't funny. At one point I slipped my hand over the bucket seat and across to hers, and we held hands for the rest of the night. I had an erection just from that touch and her vanilla perfume.*

July 12, 1992...*The summer has so much energy, and the rest of it is spread out. I kissed her. I kissed Jenny and it was beautiful and disgusting but disgusting in a beautiful way that the grossness didn't matter. Her boobs touched me through her Sonic Youth t-shirt. We kissed in the woods behind her mom's apartment building and it was dark out even though it wasn't late. My lips ache, and the skin around my mouth feels chafed, and I still smell like her on my clothes. Oh, it is beautiful.*

And I was so drunk. My eyelids were heavy and my watch said it was four-forty because it was in my line of sight on the floor. The darkness was dark...and the carpet was carpet...Jenny was here soon, and I was practicing Dawn Ego songs in my head.

The Dawn Ego's guitars whined and... Jenny. We would...I would beat her in trivia and take her ni... I would take her nipples into my mouth and see her smile and hear her... I did it in my mind, in the darkness awash with green letters on the computer screen, and as I suckled and held her breast I cried.

I cried and the cold tears pooled in the dips of my eye because my face was on the carpet and the tear had nowhere to go.

I envisioned turning my face in her lap.

I tasted her, the feel of her skin after she shaved herself, and the folds of skin in between her legs. I would hear her moan and smell her on my fingers for days.

I was crying, and drunk, and everything spun, and all I wanted was my mouth on her and making her come.

We wouldn't be...We'd be... Quiet...

...

...The hands seemed to come out of the darkness and I felt them moving around my body. Arms wrapped around my trunk, lifting me upright, and a grunt, and I helped a little with my arms as I was moved into my chair but my neck told me that my head weighed a thousand pounds and everything spun. It lolled along on a pivot and spun with the room. I opened my eyes, but whoever was manhandling me pushed me from behind in my motorized chair. Good luck, fucker.

I smelled vomit and my armpits. Vomit in my armpits.

Band name, "The Vomit Parapets."

Blurrily, bushy hair tousled down around to the front of my chair.

"Todd! Todd!" A few smacks to my face popped my eyes open. He spoke in a loud register to get through to me. "You're a mess, man. What, did you hit your head? You... Two black eyes. I am running a bath but I don't know how this stair thing works so I need a little help. I can't carry you downstairs."

The young voice. Chuck. Teenaged lead singer coming over for... to see me? Did they have practice? To give me a bath?

I popped the chair into my lift by pulling back on the joystick. I didn't buckle in. I didn't feel like explaining how to do it, and I'd be fine. The second I clicked in, the chair moved slowly down and I struggled to stay awake. I drifted off until the 'beep' at the bottom of the stairs jolted my eyes open and one of my eyes was crooked and I just wanted to go back to sleep, but it all didn't make sense.

I remembered listening to my fifteen year old self talk about Jenny, her smile, her fresh and clean and everything perfect body, and how she lived for nothing else but me, and oh, and oh, and oh, I started to cry again. Me. My drunk self, me. Mr. Piece Of Shit, me.

There was a kick, a click, and I started moving. Another hand was on my joystick, guiding my throne of dirt into the bathroom. Running water echoed through my mind, and towels were spread over the floor. The room was warm, and the red heat lamp radiated infrared over the rising dunes and dips of terrycloth.

Dozy and woozy, arms hooked under my own and pivoted me down onto the towels. I was stripped. Cold where my shit and my piss and my puke caked and chafed me. Warming under the lamp, it improved.

The faucet was shut, and the comforting sound of cupping and sloshing water. A facecloth was prepped like mother, and warmth as I was toweled down, toweled down, cool, warmth, and the sense that I was caked in shit and feeling intense natural humanness wallowing in my own filth, but now cleaned.

My eyes focused on Chad - no, Chuck; it is Chuck - as he unhooked the ports on my broken bags and figured out how to replace them with the new ones from the neat vinyl stack in the towel closet.

My eyes rolled.

He lifted me, and eased me into the warm tub. I dozed in my womblike warm water.

He gathered the towels.

I dozed.

I heard the washing machine running.

I heard the cup cup of the bathwater on the corners of the tub, and my body.

I dozed.

I woke to the tinkle of the unplugged electric guitar being played on the toilet.

I dozed.

The water came to my chin. For what would normally be a fatal bathing choice for a paralytic, I hadn't felt this relaxed in ages. Warmth. Total, encompassing warmth.

My modesty didn't bother me. I felt trusted, respected, and cared for. It was the first time I had been this comfortable since my parents lived in this house. I wanted it to last.

I looked around. Chuck fiddled with his guitar and wrote in a notebook, oblivious to my consciousness and the penis bobbing in the tides.

A glass of sweaty ice water stood with a straw on the lip of the tub. I took a sip. It made my burning throat feel better. My headache leaked a little farther down my spine from its nest on the crown of my head. It leaked away to my sour stomach, and sloshed in my feet.

I studied Chuck over the lip of the tub. His hair hung over his face as he moved the pen across the page. He would write, strum or pick a few notes, and write.

I remembered. He came to pick up his pedal. Then he saved me from choking on my own vomit. Then he used his time to work. His optimistic youth bled from his body like the condensation that collected on the side of my glass. It atomized. I could breathe it.

There was something so beautiful about watching him work, unaware that I was watching. The same young man in the same moment of his life as I was. He wanted to push against the world, in hopes that he could break through the other side in the same way I did. This young man had no idea about the arrogance and ignorance that I could see in myself in hindsight. He was ready to put everything he had into his work because that's all he knew.

I wondered. His pristine, unbroken heartbeat. Was there a Jenny in his life? The game is fixed for him, as it was for me. But, there was something for him to achieve. I wasn't holed up in an estate of despair, wanting to ruin him to make everyone as miserable as I was. He had a chance. My estate and my prison were built on these legs and that chair.

There was such potential energy stored up in that brain, in those strings, in that hand, and through that pencil. We were almost there.

I opened my mouth to say something, retched, and threw up yellow into the water.

Chapter 24

"You really don't need to do that," Chuck said as he buttoned my flannel at the kitchen table.

He got me out of the tub, dried me off, helped me situate and dress myself. He managed to keep me from hitting my head and drowning in a shallow puddle, and I learned relatively quickly that Thom's PT and OT neglected extreme drunken stumbling.

"Chuck, I have time and I have money... Just, allow me." I wanted to pay for his college. I wanted to do anything he needed. I saw more than myself in him. What teenager spends a night - a school night - changing and cleaning a man after his colostomy bag burst all over him.

New band name: Devil's Piñata.

"Okay, okay," I changed the subject, talking slowly.

"When are you guys coming over for practice, again? I am ready to put copy together for you and get some press kits going..."

"I think Friday was the plan. We've been getting together every night this week so that when we came - hey, are you still okay?" My stomach felt a sponge squeezing out green, but I nodded and powered through it. "The idea was that when we came Friday, we'd have a show together and you'd just give us improvements. I didn't say anything because I wanted to be professional about it and come with a whole set."

"Perfect. I could even start to try to get you guys a show. Don't forget that I'm here to take care of anything you need."

The conversation paused, and we looked at the table. Chuck tossed his pencil across the page.

"What time is it?"

"Eight-thirty."

"When did you get here?"

"Four thirty, quarter of five. I texted mom and said I wasn't going to be home until later - that I was here."

"You hungry?"

We ordered Chinese food and Chuck helped change the laundry and clean up my bedroom before the driver came.

We ravenously tore into the delivery. The fatty, caloric food settled my mind and my stomach. It was perfect.

"So if I hear you guys on Friday and everything sounds good, do you want to set up some dates in a week somewhere? Would you be ready?"

"Absolutely."

"...I'll make posters and get the bass head done. Everything will be clean. I already have some logo ideas."

"That sounds great - we have a ton of stuff up on Twitter and Facebook and YouTube already - we have a few thousand followers, but I'm pretty sure they're mostly our classmates. Anyway, they know our sound and our music already. We've been filming everything, taking pictures, editing down our recordings. Can I take a look at your logos?"

I rode over to the desk off the living room and grabbed my notes. I created a logo that looked somewhat like our old one, an octopus with snakes for tentacles and at its center a head with bloody eyes. It was a little Octopussy, a little Oedipus, a little Dawn Ego.

Chuck's eyes lit up.

"It's perfect. I can't wait until they see it!" he took out his phone, snapped a picture, ant tapped on the device. "Can I take this and have a friend get it on the computer and clean it up?"

"Of course!" I couldn't believe the effort he had put into everything. His resourcefulness surpassed mine. My 1994 marketing strategy was no match for what he was doing online. Was I even helping? I was a newspaper advertisement for their appearance on Laurence Welk.

"We'll still come on Friday. I know you'll have some notes, but we want to make sure it's perfect. Really. We want to show you a new set with only a few seconds between songs, and a performance so tight we can say that we have exactly whatever minutes of music. Just like you said.

"We'll be ready to play a week from Friday, though," he continued. "If you set something up, we can be here every night next week to get ready. Is that okay?"

I smiled and nodded.

We drank the soothing oolong tea bags they sent in the bag. This young man came into my life exactly when I needed him, and perhaps that's why people have children. If I had a kid in my mid-twenties, he would be around this age. He was a companion, someone to guide and watch over, and someone to teach me things about the world that I knew nothing about.

"I listened to the radio the other day," I began, "and I couldn't believe the junk that was on there. Where do you guys-"

"No one listens to the radio. It's all on the Internet. The radio has always been run by what other people think you should listen to, right? It is old technology. On the Internet, anyone can be successful."

"True. So, an old guy like me? I mean, I went to the library and took out some CDs."

"I'll make you a CD, how's that?"

I paused.

"You're a really good kid, Chuck.

"When you came tonight, I was... I went to the library today to get a new library card and check some things out, but..." I wasn't really connecting any of my ideas and how to communicate what I was trying to say.

"Before I got into my accident I had a band, and a girlfriend Jenny." He nodded. We had been over this. I choked back emotion. "I found out today...that she was dead. It happened while I was in my coma. So didn't my parents. Everyone I love. So, as I stared down at her head stone... I had some whiskey and made my way home. Drunk. The world spun, and my chair fell in the street, and I didn't give a shit.

"I forgot you were coming over. You're so selfless and for a kid your age to take care of me is just - I was never like that. You are really an incredible young man, Chuck. I look forward to everything."

He listened, and nodded. He was silent. Humble.

We cleaned up from dinner, and Chuck left.

Over the next three days I called around to set everything up. Posters and shirts with a day's turnaround once we had final logos and layouts were all set for Friday. I called possible venues, and set up a show the following Friday at the Shanghai Chinese Food Restaurant and Buffet, a large restaurant that was coincidentally built in a development a block from the bridge of my fateful accident. The Shanghai had a bar with a stage and a PA system, and all we'd have to do is show up with our gear.

I managed to get another gig for them in two weeks at another bar and restaurant called The Strand. I also called three venues in Boise and invited them to the gigs to see if they were interested in a booking.

It was easy selling people on something that doesn't exist when the product is already perfect, especially with a few white lies and the Internet.

On Thursday, Thom and Susan came for my appointment,

and the three of us sat around the table in the kitchen.

"What the hell happened to your face?" Thom was rightly concerned as he examined my fresh bruises and lacerations.

"I was trying to navigate my way on the sidewalks to the library. My chair tipped and I face planted into the pavement. Those sidewalks are terrible, but I was already on my way back, so-"

"Why were you doing that?" Susan replied. "I am supposed to bring you wherever you need to go."

"I can't rely on everybody all the time, Susan. I'm here alone most of the day. But, I'm grateful. Thank you."

"Honestly Todd, we could set you up with the Trans and their handicapped shuttle. The state pays for all this."

"I'm fine. I just want to learn how to manage."

"You are stubborn as hell, you know that?" She paused. "I brought your groceries - I put them on the landing there when I came in. Do you need anything else, or do you want to just start seeing how many shopping bags you can pack onto your chair before it tips over and you hit your head and kill yourse-"

"I'll be fine, Susan. Thank you for the groceries. I don't think I need anything else."

"It smells like liquor," Susan said to me as Thom looked at the ceiling.

"I'm sure it does."

She stood, collecting her purse and her windbreaker.

"Well, I will see you next week, and in the meantime don't kill yourself? I guess I'll call you every day to see if you need anything, and we can go from there. I need a record that you are taking care of yourself and that at least I'm trying..."

She turned and made her way out.

Thom's bulk at the small Formica table in the kitchen was comical. I would almost need to remodel the entire house to get it out of the seventies, but it was utilitarian, and it worked.

Thom started to put the groceries away for me.

"Did you drink all of that whiskey I brought over?"

"I - I had a bender the other day - on Monday - but I have an excuse.

"Remember when you told me to write letters, especially those I didn't plan on sending? When you brought the mail in the other day, you brought in my letter that I sent. It was returned.

"I went to the library. The librarian looked my parents up and told me the funeral home where they were taken, and then she was able to take the envelope and look Jenny up. I learned Jenny was dead. The love of my adolescent self was dead, and then everyone was dead around me, and everything was shit.

"So I got drunk. I fell over. I promise, the sidewalk part was real." I tried to be honest and forthright.

"No, I believe you on that."

"Yeah, the only thing is that when you land on your face, this happens."

"So what are you doing besides trying to kill yourself?"

"Did I tell you about the kids in the band?"

"A little."

"Coincidentally one of them came over after my chair

crash and helped me get my shit together, literally. My bag broke, and Susan would have been a lot of help cleaning the shit off of me, but..." Thom laughed. "Thankfully, the boy from the band is this really nice kid. He cleaned me up and got me together · which was fate considering he accidentally left something at my house. I bought us some Chinese food and we had a good night after that.

"I'm getting them ready to play a show. I would love you to be there if you aren't busy. It's a week from Friday at the Shanghai."

"I think I'll do that. Friday and Saturday are the music nights in the bar?" Thom asked.

"Exactly. Friday night at eight. Bring everyone."

Thom slowed down and looked at me as if to ask everything was really, truly, okay. I hope I communicated back with my eyes that it wasn't, but that I would survive.

"Well, at least you have someone to keep you in bourbon for a while," he finally said.

"True." The sneaking suspicion that I shouldn't be drinking as much as I have rose in my gut. I wasn't much of a drinker for my first forty or so years. Thom's approach to taking care of me as a man and a peer was much more effective than what everyone else did. I had a spinal injury two decades ago, not a brain injury.

"You're taking the initiative, man. Following your passions again," Thom continued. "That's the quickest way to normal that exists. Your spirit is stronger than ever. You want to survive, and you are proving it by taking up your work again. That works better than any of the exercises and skills I am paid to do with you, and way better than any treatment, medication, or chemical. Passion."

"I'm trying," I responded.

"If you feel like I am too much, just let me know."

"Susan is a bit much. She'd be fine if she didn't talk."

"I know."

"You are great, Thom. I look forward to our visits. You have a lot of great things to say."

"Thanks."

"Can I ask you an easy favor?" I continued. I handed him the obituaries. "Do you think you could swing by here and ask about my parents, where they are buried, whatever information they have? Tell them they can call me at their old number if they need permission, or anything. I don't think I can bring myself to do it."

"I will. I need to leave, but I'll call you if I need anything for your parents." Thom stood and put his jacket on. "You probably learned more in that one field trip to the library than I could teach you in six months."

"I think you're right. I learned a hell of a lot."

"Take care, Todd. Don't hesitate to holler if you need anything else. I'll see you and your boys at the show on Friday."

Thom left.

Silence.

There was so much to do, and all the time in the world to

do it.

That was one major difference between my adolescent and modern self. In my teenage years I had the optimism, drive, and creativity of a thousand men, little time and money to execute everything. In adulthood, I had the time and money to follow my passions to the end of the earth, but my creativity and drive was as dead as any fortysomething.

While I drowned in adulthood as a paraplegic rocker, it was time to sow the seeds of my boys and help them reap the success I never had in this world that I knew so little about.

Friday approached.

As much as I wanted to indulge, I avoided my computer journals and the bottle. I just focused on doing my best work with what time I had. Chuck and I used his tablet to send some incredible poster designs to the printer. He also showed me his work on the internet. There were certain websites and social sites that were imperative. Everything with the logo and the band photos looked sharp, and close to fifteen thousand followers kept tabs on them between the Facebook, the YouTube, the Twitter, SoundCloud, and a variety of other platforms.

"They are mostly from the high school, though, and they overlap," he commented.

"I don't care - that's a real number, man."

"I would love to bring you your own tablet and give you access to all of this so you can post updates and stuff - that is the real key. Update and stay relevant."

"I could write copy forever, and I have the time to do it,

but you don't need to do that."

"Perfect. No worries, Todd. I'll get you one. They're cheap."

The rest of the guys arrived, and I had Chuck help me down to the basement. I had a schedule for the week planned out.

I told them for the first rehearsal that they should pretend I wasn't there, and just run through their set.

They played magnificently. It was tight, and the only immediate worry was to curate the songs by editing them from the nineteen they had down to a manageable ten or twelve and keep the entirety of the set at a little bit less than an hour. We'd plan an encore, whether there was one or not.

The first show was fifty-six minutes of music, with just under fifteen minutes of encore. We wrote it out...

1. Intro.

2. Vascular

3. Slap shop.

4. The Defeated I Know

5. My Heart is A Finch In The Dusk

6. Disease

7. Fishing for Breath

8. Lights

9. Nothing to Do

10. 42

11. Conclusion.

Encore 1: Just For Me

Encore 2: Belief

Encore 3: A Day / The End

Their assignment for Saturday was to practice through the list and to think through where they could find a spot to surreptitiously tune throughout the set. They would also pick up the shirts and posters, and plaster the city on their way over.

Before they arrived on Saturday, I called The Shanghai and convinced them to switch the show to eighteen-plus and charge a cover to the minors. They asked to keep the cover money. I asked to keep all merchandise profits. We made a deal.

Saturday night's rehearsal was perfect. The band played through their entire set, and the only issues I saw with the actual show was their execution two tune up areas. We solved those with a bass and drums loop while the tune up happened on the stage. Only seconds separated each song. Everything was clean.

I asked them to arrive to the next rehearsal in what they were planning on wearing at the show. They also had to bring a few different pieces along in case they didn't cut it.

Sunday was for style.

While I knew nothing about contemporary style, I tried to take a page from what they brought to manufacture an edgy look to their brand. They wouldn't cut it with flannel, as much as I wanted them to. There was no doubt, however, that picking the tightest fitting jeans for each of them would still make a good base no matter what era this was.

They came in fluorescent red and yellow pants, and they insisted on wearing bright, lens-less wayfarers. Geek hard rockers seemed to work. I combed their hair over their faces. Chuck grabbed an old black eyeliner pencil from my bedroom.

We pushed back to the nineties in a fashion that was applicable, tasteful, and provocative to such an extent that I couldn't take my eyes off of them.

Their show was somewhat boring, though, and Monday's rehearsal we would be for working through the technical performance. I taught them body language, stances, and basic choreography to engage the crowd.

Monday and Tuesday were awash with suggestions, emotions, how to talk, and carriage for on and off stage. I had to teach them what it means to be in character, what it means to rock, and define what it means to be Oedipussy.

The played, and I cut them off.

Once, it was "put your foot on the monitor, there, and show the audience note bending by wiggling your hand just so," and often I found myself shouting over their music, "You know the song! Stop looking at your guitar!"

When we began, they performed as awkwardly as they carried themselves.

"You are not robots, you are rock stars. Fuck the man, fuck the police - you aren't children! You're the captains of the world! The leaders of the universe! You're holding on to the vibrations and the sound of everything! Play like it!"

I forced them to play a song three times, and at other times I would take the camera they used to record everything and play back what they just did in front of them.

"Look at this shit! Does this look exciting? Do you look like you are owning this? Or is it more like you aren't sure if mom is going to come downstairs and tell you to turn down?"

They improved drastically.

"Your audience is going to have as much energy and excitement as the show they are going to see. If you play a sit down show, they are going to be a sit down audience. If you bring the electricity - truly bring everything you possibly can and get people on their feet, smiling, and excited for what you are doing, they will meet you there. Even if there's only two people! That is your mission Friday night."

I hammered them for hours, and they had one job for Wednesday. They had to show me the show they were planning on playing on Friday without any feedback from me. We were going to film it, and they could watch it on their own. They had forty-eight hours before the show, and they could watch it forty times.

The only instructions for Thursday were: meditate, reflect, focus, and prepare.

Wednesday was magical. It was momentous, strong, and they clearly worked on their image and performance between rehearsals. I was sure there would be many minute things that the boys were going to take care of after watching the video, but at the same rate I could find very little about their performance that I would change.

Watching them, I enjoyed myself. I felt the thumping magic of their presence as they worked through their set. There was no question that they would be performing their encore.

On Thursday, Susan brought me to the print shop. Against Chuck's advice, I got them to quickly engineer and rush order as many CDs as they could make before the show and deliver them to the venue by six so we had something to sell besides shirts.

Thursday night in bed, I relented.

I understood what was in my control, and what wasn't.

I gave up trying to prepare, and I hoped the boys were studying and preparing.

I hoped everything was going to work.

I hoped it would be the best concert that Twin Falls ever had, and that her audience would revel in our work.

I hoped that art and beauty would be synonymous with our show.

Everything would begin the following night.

Friday.

I lay awake looking at the daubed plaster ceiling, hoping in the darkness.

I hoped until the sun crept up.

Chapter 25

The Shanghai was as an opulent pageant of Oriental design. It was two stories tall, and took up an entire city block. It was more spectacle than restaurant, with live music, an exciting hibachi, a luxurious buffet, the best hospitality in town, and delicious authentic food.

Tonight, it was our palatial arena.

I sat arranging the merchandise table while the band loaded their gear onto the stage through door behind a big drape in the lounge. They were professional, their attention directed entirely on their silent teamwork. Watching them made me nostalgic for The Dawn Ego's historic coffee shop load in.

The printer delivered a hundred and fifty CDs to me at the table. It was more than I was expecting, but I wasn't concerned about being able to sell them. I fanned them on the table with the shirts.

Oedipussy was one, and they were real. It shone off the microphones, and off the Octopus Oedipus Ouroboros on the bass drum head. We were making magic in this small pond. In Shanghai.

Chuck ran to my table at the front of the room.

"Hey. Looks like we're all set. Can we do a sound check with you up here?"

I wheeled to the man on the sound board. The band ran through their instruments and vocals. I helped the man tweak. They tweaked. Everything seemed so easy, but perhaps that's what comes from so much preparation that everyone would be ready at the actual event.

The boys may have been nervous, but I couldn't tell. I was surprised at how little concern I had. I knew they would be excellent.

They finished their song with a few minor tweaks, but they were perfect.

I met the boys at the back of the bar.

"What time is it?" I asked.

"It is seven forty five. Fifteen minutes until door."

It had come to this.

"Do you guys have everything you need?"

"Yeah. We do," Chuck replied.

"Water?"

"The bar is passing it up on to the stage as we go."

"I noticed it's a little cool right now, but I'm sure it'll heat up once you're jumping around and the bodies get in here. Do you need towels?"

"That isn't a bad idea..."

"Okay, I'll ride across the street and get you some at the sports store there. They should still be open. We still have forty five minutes."

Chang, the tuxedoed owner of the restaurant, came over to discuss how we wanted the performance to go. He personally wanted to introduce the band at eight thirty, and to assure us that his bartenders and doormen were all set to take care of the ticketing and merchandise. Everything would be tracked and taken care of before they left, including Chang deciding to add an unexpected twenty percent of the bar and door revenue back to the band.

"We want you to come back. You are very nice young men. We are excited about the online response," Chang told us. "Very good marketing for you and for the Shanghai."

The boys thanked him and shook his hand. As Chang walked away, we rejoiced.

"I'm going to go get you those towels," I said. "You guys make sure you have everything you need set up, and I'll meet you at the back door when I come back." They nodded.

The lounge wasn't open yet, so the boys brought me down through the back. While the room was huge, the geography of the building was confusing. I was surprised that we were still level with the pavement at the back of the room as with the front. I easily rolled out onto the street through the stage doors.

I turned. Pools of street light guided me up the street.

"Todd!" Thom shouted to me as he got out of his car. The engine of the little red thing clicked as it cooled. His giant mass squeezed out like gelatin.

"So glad you could make it," I said as he bent over for a bear hug.

"I wouldn't miss it. Very excited to hear your band play."

"It's not mine, Thom."

"It's your project. It's yours. They'll be excellent."

"Thank you."

"This might not be the right time, but I'm happy I caught you. I got your parents." He bent back over into his tiny car and produced two small cardboard boxes.

I looked at my mom and dad's names. They were typed onto cards. The cards were pasted to the cardboard boxes resting in his meaty hands under a streetlight. I held my hands out.

"Thank you."

He stood in silence, I sat.

What do you say in times like these?

"I can't wait to hear what you think," I offered.

"I better get up there for a good spot," he joked, jutting his chin toward the restaurant. A serpentine line curved along the building and down the street. Their audience was going to be An Audience.

"Thom," I said. "Thank you."

I rode two blocks up the street to the used sporting goods store, Twice As Nice. I bought six fresh white towels for the boys.

I headed back with my parents on my lap.

The line was even longer. Countless college-aged kids shifted in the cool night air.

I rode down the street and behind the building to the double stage doors. I was greeted by the boys and their families. Their smiles beamed.

"Everything you've done for these boys is incredible," Chuck's mother said. "I was skeptical, but in all sincerity I have seen such a change in Chuck over the last few weeks. They are better musicians and better boys now, because of you." I tried to keep my composure as I was introduced to Mark and Adam's parents and was greeted with more striking praise. I've never been thanked so wonderfully.

They hugged their children, turned, and entered the lounge together. Peeking through the doors as they entered, my line of sight was blocked by a wall of people. The room was packed.

Chang emerged through the doors.

"You guys ready in five?"

The boys nodded. I handed Chang the towels.

"When you go in, could you could toss two of these next to each of the boys' instruments?"

Chang obliged and disappeared back through the open doors with the towels.

I put my hands out beside me. My mother and father slept on my lap.

Chuck took my right hand, Mark took my left, and Adam

joined everyone together.

"Tonight is the real beginning," I began. "The beginning of Oedipussy. Most bands have some strange growing pains, problems, personalities; but it's incredible that three men were able to come together to create something magic in the short amount of time you have. Management and guidance is just a way to make sure you're your best selves - but as musicians, friends, coworkers, social media campaigners... You guys have so much talent and skill that I feel like I did so little...

"Thank you for inviting me and allowing me to be a part of your work and your world over the last couple months to help you put this together. I'm an old, broken man. I could never do this. When I was your age, there's nothing I would have wanted to do more than be here with you tonight. Since I can't go back, and since I am who I am, and since you are who you are, helping you be the best that you can be is enough. Your music... your success... this is enough for me."

I felt our hands get tighter, and tighter as I spoke. We strengthened our grip into one force. Here we were. We were more in the now than ever.

"We can't thank you enough," Mark said.

"You're a real mentor and leader," Adam responded.

"This has been the best time of my life, making art with you," Chuck finished.

We released our grip. One by one, the boys knelt to hug me, and they hugged each other. I would have killed them if they let anyone see them do this to their image as a band, but my heart leapt in my chest at the camaraderie and love they shared.

As we embraced, everything became a hush on the other side of the doors. The roar of glasses stopped clinking, the ambient music faded out, and the energetic buzz of the crowd dissipated. There was silence.

"Ladies and Gentlemen," Chang began, "welcome to Twin Falls' most beautiful venue for live music and home of authentic Schezuan, Cantonese, Hunan, and Hibachi cuisine." We broke our embrace, and the palpable electricity arced on the hairs on the back of our necks. The boys slowly walked toward the doors. "They are making waves on the Internet, and their sound is unlike anything you've heard before..." They looked back at me, and smiled. "Ladies and Gentlemen, The Shanghai is proud to present: Oedipussy!"

The crowd erupted. I watched as the boys bounded up to the stage, their backs bathed in dim red light.

I only followed them partway into the building. I watched from below on stage right. Hundreds of people, ecstatic and alive, stood on the precipice of the future.

Chuck approached the microphone.

Click, click, click went the drumsticks as Chuck was airborne.

His hand came down onto the strings, and white light faded in. Everyone took a breath in through their mouths, wide-wide-open.

I looked out onto the emptiness of the canyon from the bridge.

Music and excitement echoed from the open stage doors at the Shanghai not two hundred feet from where I sat in my chair.

This was the bridge our van careened off. Everyone I cared about slowly disappeared over twenty years. I've been gone.

Oedipussy was in their encore, and so was I.

Through the darkness, I focused on the expanse.

The stars opened like a dark blanket of laser beauty over my head. Below, the rocky clay pot of nothingness was barely visible. The sun's photons bounced around the earth and off the moon and back down to earth and off the rocks and into my eyes.

I stared into the void behind the guardrail, and something called to me.

I wheeled as close as I could. It seemed somewhat new, unscathed, and clean. I picked up mom and dad's boxes and put them on the railing. I put my hands on the railing, and pulled myself out of my chair and up and over the metal with my hands. My legs were wobbly beneath me, but I was able to keep still with my upper body.

I pulled myself up, extending and locking my arms on the railing, and I howled. I was a pommel horse gymnast. I was a wolf.

My back arched, and I pulled my hips above the guardrail, and up onto the second metal reinforcement. I sat. I picked my legs up and swung them around under the light of the moon.

I sat on a railing above the canyon that took me. I sat next to the ashes of my parents.

I felt so worn down.

The thumping of the song ended, and the echoes of the cheering crowd wafted on the air. Cheer. Softer, cheer. Whispercheer. Everything felt so real for the moment.

I shattered another scream that carried itself in the air and washed through the gorge. It was a word that seemed to begin as 'why' but changed into 'what' as it came out. It dissipated into the stars, and the gorge responded, '-ut,' '-ut,' '-ut,' softer and softer into nothingness.

And then I had the idea... What would happen?

Looking over the precipice into the abyss I had the urge to take one more dive. To show Mother Nature and gravity that if I could do it once, I could do it again. All that would be left is my chair, as if I never existed. It was an intense momentary magnetism; not a need to die, but a need to live.

I opened mother's box. I sloppily tore the cardboard in a half moon. There was a plastic bag with clumpy ash sand. I took the bag out and tossed the box into the canyon. I slowly poured her into the air. She became a powdery cloud, catching in the undercurrent of the breeze. Some cloud wafted into my mouth.

I dropped the bag.

I did the same for Father.

He fell like dead weight. His sand careened straight into

the blackness like a brick.

The cheering was muffled with the slamming of the double doors. I looked to the back of the restaurant. The boys spoke to one another below the service light. They hugged and celebrated, positive and joyous.

In the silence, I could barely remember the life I once led. Once, my optimism drowned negativity. When I was young I wasn't even aware of it, as if negativity wasn't even possible. When I was young I was alive. These young men were the true metamorphosis of myself. I felt alive again.

The wind blew across the bridge and against my back. It tempted my balance. It urged me to shift my weight toward the canyon. I braced against it.

I relished in watching their joy.

Chang materialized through the doors and approached the boys with a fat envelope. They had a short conversation before he went back in. The boys became even more elated, dramatically acting out the conversation with their hands. Chuck spun on his heels to search the area.

He spotted me and walked toward the bridge.

As he approached, his body darkened as he left the outlined of the service lights on the building. Every few steps he was bathed in saintly gowns of white streetlight.

"How'd it go?" I asked.

"It was incredible. The crowd was - Chang said there were three hundred and seventy five people at the show and they had to turn people away into the restaurant because there wasn't enough room · and then he said the restaurant filled up!"

"I stayed for most of the set," I said, "but it got hot by your encore, and there were too many people. I just needed some air."

I paused, and nodded toward the sky above the canyon. "The stars are beautiful," I said.

Chuck walked up to the railing and put his arms on it and searched the gorge and the sky. Sweat beaded down his skin. He took a deep breath.

"This is beautiful."

In the night, under the light of the stars, we both paused.

Water bubbled quietly below. The ambient breeze flitted through the trees, and a tiny chatter of the concertgoers' voices trailed back from their cars a couple blocks away. All sound dissipated into the night sky. The air was clean and remarkable.

"You feel good?" I asked.

"Chang gave us an envelope. It has nine hundred bucks in it. That was just cut of our bar share, and he also let us keep the cover charge money. He thought it wasn't right to keep any of it. He told us he made a killing at dinner. He said he'll give us the merch money once we were done, and he also wants to give the four of us a dinner spread," Chuck said. "You should come back in and eat with us."

"Thanks. I will. I just want to sit here for a little while in the quiet."

"Sure... Listen, we've talked about this, and we want to give you the money from tonight·"

I began to relent, upset even that the discussion turned to

money on this beautiful night. Money was the opposite of everything I was experiencing right now. Chuck cut me off from my thoughts.

"-and we want you to know that this isn't payment or anything, but more like an investment in us. We've already spent a bunch of your cash, and we know you're making your own label and all of that, but think of it like investing in the future of Oedipussy. Really. That way, if we need strings, or a new cymbal, or stickers, or whatever, we can just come to you."

"But I was going to get that for you anyway," I responded.

"Which is exactly why what we made will go into an account with you. It can still be our money to spend on the band, just in your hands. The business."

What could I say? The little fuckers were right, and I had no right to refuse it since I was planning on spending more on them.

"Okay. But it's still your money."

"It's Oedipussy's."

I nodded.

I sat on the railing looking down, down, down into the hole where fate took me. Then, back at Chuck, and the up, up, up, of the future. Music was a glorious revelation that I was still making something happen.

"You know, this is the railing the van went over when we had the accident," I said.

"It was a beautiful night. I was playing the first show with our band. We were called 'The Dawn Ego.' Twin Falls never saw anything like this with their country bands and roadhouse cover bands... We were different. We swore we'd be the next Nirvana, or something.

"We were all packed up and this truck came out of nowhere.

"The next minute, I had this crazy dream about us becoming famous, and sex, drugs, success. More success than I could ever imagine.

"But papercut deep, just under the surface... It was this weird, twisted reality. The real reality. Twenty-five years later I wake up with hardly anything to live for."

I shifted my support corset under my shirt to the left to remove the pressure of it pinching my hip.

"I'm so grateful for you boys. Everything seems promising. It's just a coincidence that your show was here tonight, and I know you want to thank me and everything, but... You're helping. I'm being reborn from this canyon into the beauty of your music. Where you grow, so do I. I'm following you out of the wreckage, just as you're following me into the stars."

"Thank you," he said.

"Thank you," I replied.

The breeze was cool, the air was crisp and fresh.

Five minutes passed.

Ten minutes passed.

"Want to go get that dinner?" Chuck asked.

"Yeah. Go ahead. I just need a few more minutes."

Chuck walked on.

I sat on a ledge, far from my wheelchair and far from my death.

I watched the stars turn as the universe spun us into the future. We careened through the galaxy at sixty-seven thousand miles per hour.

My heart, however, leapt faster than everything.

Acknowledgements

This novel would not have been possible without the friendship, work, and brotherhood of many years with many special people.

Thank you to FortNight, our crew and guests, and our audience. Most importantly, I would like to thank Mr. Berube, Mr. Farnsworth, and Mr. Wood. Thank you also to Mike Gary, Nichole Pagnotta, and Toilet Plunger, as well as Ken McLaughlin, John Sage, Jay Tagg, J. Michael Wahlgren, and Ad Frank for many years of friendship and music.

Also, thanks to several legendary figures: Dick DiCenso, Mrs. Grigatis, Mr. LaPierre, and the great Bonney Bouley for fostering a lifelong love for the art.

FREE Oedipussy Album

As part of the release of this novel, Perpetual Imagination would like to invite you to download a free album written and recorded specifically to accompany this release!

The album is currently in production and will be released in the near future.

To reserve your free digital copy of the album when it is completed, simply visit...

http://bit.ly/oedipussydownload

...and enter your email address and Amazon order number to receive updates, join the Solomon Deep mailing list, and get your free download code!

The Typeface...

Oedipussy has been set in Century.

Century originates from a first design, Century Roman cut by American Type Founders designer Linn Boyd Benton in 1894 for master printer Theodore Low De Vinne, for use in his Century magazine. Century is based on the Scotch Roman and Scotch Modern genres, two related styles of type of British origin which had been popular in the United States from the early nineteenth century. Its design emphasizes crispness and elegance, with strokes ending in fine tapers, ball terminals and crisp, finely pointed serifs.

With the merging of twenty-three foundries into American Type Founders in 1892, Linn Boyd Benton's son, Morris Fuller Benton, was given the task of consolidating and purging the faces of these manufacturers into a coherent selection. Following this, he was given the task of adapting Century No. 2 to meet the Typographical Union standards of the time.

The Supreme Court of the United States requires that briefs be typeset in Century family type.

SOLOMON DEEP

Solomon Deep is a writer who lives in Northampton and New York.

He is best known as the writer and host of *FortNight,* a live rock and roll stage show in the style of old time radio. It's punk as fuck.

Deep also enjoys gardening, beekeeping, and acting.